THE WOMEN'S WAR

Carol Ervin

THE WOMEN'S WAR
Copyright © 2016 by Carol L. Ervin

ISBN (Paperback) : 978-1534939486

Original cover design by Valentina Migliore

To all the women of my life who've been my family and friends, mentors, students, neighbors and colleagues.
You are magnificent.

LIST OF CHARACTERS

Characters in *The Women's War* who are important in this and other books in the series, listed by first name:

Alma Donnelly: Luzanna's daughter, age 16
Barlow Townsend: husband of May Rose and father of Freddy; former superintendent of the Winkler Lumber Company, now a partner in the Winkler Mine
Blanche Cotton: daughter of Simpson Wainwright, mother of three children who are in the care of her father; wife of Raz Cotton (deceased)
Charlie Herff: ex-cowboy, now stockyard worker, brother of Will and Glory; lived with May Rose in Fargo until he was 16
Cotton brothers: Coyne, Raz, and Duck. Raz and Duck are deceased.
Emmy and **Tim Donnelly**: Luzanna's younger children
Evie Wyatt: age 14, daughter of Wanda and her first husband, Homer Wyatt
Freddy Townsend: infant son of May Rose and Barlow

Glory Townsend: Hester's adopted daughter, biological sister to Will and Charlie Herff

Hester Townsend (deceased): Barlow's sister, operator of the former Winkler boardinghouse

Homer Wyatt (deceased): Wanda's first husband

Jamie Long (deceased): May Rose's first husband; Wanda's father

John Donnelly (deceased): Luzanna's first husband; former tormenter of Wanda, May Rose, and the Herff boys (*The Girl on the Mountain*)

Lucie Bosell: Wanda's grandmother; mother of Piney, Ruth, and Wanda's mother Evalena (deceased)

Luzanna Donnelly Hale: May Rose's closest friend; wife of John Donnelly (deceased) and former common-law wife of Abner Hale

May Rose Long Townsend: wife of Barlow and mother of Freddy; stepmother of Wanda

Otis Herff: young son of Wanda and Will Herff

Piney Bosell Wainwright: Wanda's aunt; wife of Simpson Wainwright

Price Loughrie: one-time marshal; close companion of Ruth Bosell

Randolph Bell: engineer and partner in the Winkler mine with Will and Barlow

Raz Cotton (deceased); Blanche's husband

Ruby, **Robert**, and **Ralphie Cotton**: young children of Raz and Blanche, now in the care of Simpson and Piney Wainwright.

Russell Long: May Rose's brother-in-law from her first marriage; Wanda' uncle

Ruth Bosell: Wanda's aunt

Simpson Wainwright: miller, father of Blanche Cotton; married to Piney Bosell

Virgie White: young widow, friend of May Rose and Wanda

Wanda Wyatt Herff: wife of Will Herff; daughter of Evalina Bosell and Jamie Long; May Rose's stepdaughter; mother of Evie Wyatt, whose father Homer is deceased, and Otis Herff

Will Herff: Wanda's second husband; father of Otis; doctor and partner in the Winkler Mine

CHAPTER 1

That summer we worried about the wrong things. We gave no thought for the bad thing that was coming because we did not know until it was upon us. Ordinary concerns felt bad enough at the time, fears of hasty steps and stumbles and of events beyond our control that could ruin the future of those we loved.

Summer night breezes carried murmurs from house to house through open windows—a rising volume of voices, a baby's cry, the barking of dogs. The crash of something fallen. The sobbing of a wife, the curse of a man pushed beyond endurance by the strains of providing, or by drink, or both.

Often after midnight I walked my baby among crates of furniture in the unfinished front rooms of our house and jiggled him at the windows, looking down at Winkler, inviting him to appreciate the dots of light that looked like spots of hope. Sometimes I said a prayer, because lights in the small hours usually signaled someone's distress. There was always sickness and loss.

For me, too much was untried. I was a new wife and mother in a town built up and occupied almost overnight. All that excitement came with a new set of concerns.

CAROL ERVIN

Once or twice each night I slid from bed and bent over Freddy's crib, trying to detect the sound of his breath. In the months before he was born, I'd feared he would come out dead, like Barlow's son with his first wife, or that I would die in childbirth, like my mother. I confided these fears only to my friend Luzanna, who promised that if I went the way of my mother, she and all my friends would help Barlow raise the baby. She did not try to convince me all would be well, for such a promise would seem like inviting fate to prove her wrong.

When Freddy was born perfect in every way, I worried his father and I would not live to see him grow up. We were old to be raising our first child—Barlow was 54 and I was 38.

Freddy was a colicky baby. Through weeks in which I lived unconscious of the date or day, I walked him round and round the two finished rooms of our house, but seldom outside, where flies buzzed in the heat and coal dust rose in a cloud with every passing wagon. Having the baby always in my arms, I failed even as a housewife of two rooms. Luzanna baked our bread, washed Freddy's diapers and ironed Barlow's shirts. Everyone said the baby was healthy, though he cried all day long. I worried he was trying to tell us about some terrible pain. I worried I was losing my mind.

I felt selfish, concentrating on Freddy to the exclusion of everything else, but I could not admit to my friends that my baby ruled. He'd changed me in other ways, like my tastes for food. When I was expecting, I'd craved beets and carrots, Barlow's favorites. "This baby is turning me into you," I told him. We laughed about that. Giving birth turned me into someone else: Freddy's mother. Nursing made me hungry and exhausted, and after a day of his crying, I was sure he was no more ready to be my child than I was prepared to be his mother.

I was little help to my husband, who had a new and difficult job of his own. He returned for lunch every day, often to fry his own slice of ham. Then he would put a clean diaper over his shoulder and take Freddy from my arms. The baby, who seemed to notice this change, would stop crying for a blessed few minutes, reinforcing my fear that I was bad for him. If he started to fuss again, Barlow would fetch Freddy's bonnet and carry him outside, leaving me too frazzled to protest but selfishly pleased by the sudden stillness in the house. I missed the quiet mornings we'd shared before Freddy's birth. I worried I might come to resent them both.

Advice from my friends did not help.

"May Rose, it's okay to let the baby cry," Luzanna said, but only once, for she was not a nag.

My stepdaughter, Wanda, didn't mind being a nag. "Ma, leave him be, he'll get tired of crying. Put that baby down. You're keeping him awake." In my estimation, Wanda did not give enough attention to her own boy Otis, now going on three and forever exploring and toppling everything he could reach.

I tried not to depend too much on Luzanna, who supported her family by doing chores for others like cleaning and taking in washing.

"Think how sad you'll be when Freddy leaves for his first day of school," she said. "Imagine him grown up, an important man. None o'my kids think they need me anymore. Sometimes it makes me sad."

I thought I could manage better if I were younger.

"You took care of hundreds of babies in the orphanage," Wanda said.

Luzanna thought that might be my trouble. "You just know too much. It's best to have your first when you're young and ignorant of all the bad that could happen."

I could not pretend to know more about bad times than Luzanna. When we'd met, she and her children had been starving.

As a partner in the Winkler Mine, my husband had his own set of challenges, but with me he shared only his concerns for our family. He had a special worry for Glory, who'd grown up in his home, the adopted daughter of his sister. Like a father, Barlow wanted to see Glory well and safely married, but to his mind she was in danger of ruining herself by being the friend of Virgie White.

Glory was the youngest in my circle of friends. Unlike the rest of us, she'd finished high school, and she'd also studied art for a year in Richmond. She seemed an odd companion for Virgie, who was at least ten years older, a widow, poorly educated, and by most standards, less than respectable.

Barlow had difficulty restraining himself when Glory rented a room in Virgie's house. "She should be with us," he said. "I'll find some way to finish a room for her."

I was proud of Glory, who'd grown from a neglected infant into an accomplished woman. For Barlow's sake, I tried to explain away her reluctance to live with us. "I see no sign of her following Virgie's ways—it's Virgie's dressmaking and fashion sense she admires. I think they plan and sew every hour of the day."

I didn't tell him that Luzanna said Glory and Virgie were as confident and ambitious as men. I also didn't tell him that behind Virgie's back, Wanda called her the black widow. For all I knew, she said it to her face too.

❧

That summer Luzanna shared her fears for her elder daughter. "May Rose, Alma's got me beside myself," she said, coming into my kitchen on an ordinary sweaty morning with a stack of clean diapers. She spoke softly, looking about for Freddy, who was usually fussing in my arms.

I immediately worried too, because Alma was not the kind of girl to give trouble. "Freddy's asleep," I said, crossing my fingers.

Luzanna stood like she was trying to decide where she was. "Let me give a hand with these dishes," she said.

"No, not now. He wakes at the slightest clink." I found an uncluttered spot on the table to set the diapers, then poured two glasses of tea. "Let's talk outside."

We took our tea to the wooden table and benches under the sugar maple. Luzanna clutched the glass with reddened fingers while I prepared to be strong for her sake.

She wiped sweat from the glass and swiped its wetness across her forehead. "May Rose, what should I tell Alma about men? All these new boys are turning her head. I'm afraid she's about as ignorant of all that as I was."

I knew what she meant by *all that*, compulsions we did not understand or speak of, the kind that could so easily lead to unhappy consequences. Luzanna had buried one husband, escaped the second, and lost three of her six children. I'd had the misfortune to meet her husbands, both wretched choices. But Alma must know something of *all that*. She was sixteen now, a good girl, and a delight to see. Her mother had good reason to worry—with the new mines, Winkler was too full of rough men and boys. Even so, her mother's experiences might have made Alma wary of men, especially if she had any memory of her own pa.

"What does she remember about her father?"

"I'm sure she remembers him shoving me around. Or trying. Much as I could, I shoved back."

We were only the two of us in the yard, and there were no neighboring houses near, but Luzanna lowered her voice. "Alma don't know it, but John Donnelly wasn't her real pa—I was in the family way when I married him. At the time, him coming along with an offer seemed a lucky thing, so you see how wrong I've been most of my life. It might be hard to believe, but I was pretty like Alma a long time ago, and you know if a girl lets a boy get real close she's liable to lose her senses and not fight him off when he tries to get a hand in her bloomers. Her real pa's name was Foster. I don't even remember the rest, except he lit out when I told him Alma was on the way."

I was relieved to know that Alma's father was not John Donnelly. Wanda and I had never told Luzanna how well we'd known her husband and his brother, bullies who'd terrorized Winkler when it was a logging town. And we'd agreed with our husbands, who'd known the Donnellys too, that the sins of the father need not pass to their children. Luzanna's younger children bore both the Donnelly name and look, though fortunately not their bad manners.

"Tell Alma about her real pa," I said.

"I'm ashamed I don't remember much. I was such a stupid girl."

"He must have seemed wonderful. Handsome, kind. Entertaining."

"I suppose he was."

"The kind of boy everyone likes, but he likes you best. Or maybe he doesn't like you best and you want him to."

Luzanna gave me a long sideways look. "Sounds like you knew the like."

"He sounds like Jamie Long, my first husband," I said. "When I married him I had no idea he was Wanda's father."

"You and Wanda never say a word about him. Does he never cross your mind?"

"Sometimes. Much as I'd like to rid myself of the past, it's not easy, is it?"

"'Deed it ain't. Virgie said Wanda's pa never married her mother, but you know how Virgie is. I never know how much to believe of what she says. Is it true he murdered a man?"

"It's true Jamie never married Wanda's mother, and he did kill a man. It was a fight." I waited for her to ask if the man he'd killed was John Donnelly's pa, but perhaps Virgie had withheld that part of the story.

"And died in a train wreck, did he?"

"A terrible death," I said.

"Wanda never talks about the old times except to tell some story that makes us laugh. Did Virgie know Wanda's pa?"

"It's likely Virgie heard about Jamie before she met us; she grew up not far from here, and you know how people talk—anything with a hint of scandal spreads faster than good news. When I was married to Jamie there was talk about me too, untrue and unkind. But think about Alma, now. Tell her how you were sure her father was a perfect boy. Tell her how some men can fool us into thinking there's a good side to them. Tell her it can take a year or more of marriage to know if he's true or false. If you want, I'll tell her the whole truth about Jamie and me."

"I'd be grateful, for she looks up to you. One of these days when your baby's in a good mood, I'll send her over for a talk."

"Oh, tell her to come anytime." Freddy hadn't given me a good day since his birth.

杓杓

BEFORE MINING COMPANIES CAME TO WINKLER, GATHERING with my friends was frequent and spontaneous, but a larger population had somehow restricted our meeting to a specific place and time. Virgie had the most pleasant parlor, and she liked to entertain, so for the past year our small sewing circle had met there on Saturday afternoons. After Freddy was born, I tried to take him with me, but Barlow soon sympathized and took over his care at those times. I needed to advise Alma to find a man who would surprise her in good ways like that.

At a Saturday meeting in the midst of that summer's heat wave, Glory shared her worries about the river. On hot afternoons, splashing in the river's deep pools was the favorite entertainment of local boys.

Like Virgie, Glory was free with her opinions, which included concern for the poverty and health of the miners' wives and children. "The children shouldn't swim in the river when it's low like this," Glory said. "You smell it, don't you?"

"I can't keep my boy out of it," Luzanna said. "There's cleaner pools in streams off the hills but they're dried up now."

The Winkler Mine had a bathhouse with hot and cold water for the miners, and Glory had influenced Barlow and his partners to let the children cool off there. But only the girls and their mothers took advantage of the bathhouse; the boys preferred the allure of the river's pools and rocks. Glory had stood up in church one Sunday and talked about upstream privies built too close to the riverbanks. She said if mothers couldn't keep their kids out of the river, they must tell them never to let its water into their mouths. Barlow told me he could see the mothers thought this young woman knew nothing about the inclinations of boys.

Glory also worried about rats, the trash dump where the older ones played, and the threat of privies contaminating our wells.

Threats to the children's health seemed to me a proper cause for concern, but Wanda, who'd had more than her share of desperate times, thought Glory was worrying about nothing. "They may be poor, but they live in good new houses. The kids will be fine as long as they've got a good ma or pa."

Glory's own mother might have been a good one, but she'd died when Glory was a baby, and her father had left her in the care of her brothers, just children themselves. In those days, Barlow managed the Winkler Logging and Lumber Company, and his sister Hester ran the boardinghouse where they lived. Hester adopted Glory when she was just a toddler. If Barlow and Hester had continued to live in Winkler after the timber played out, Glory would have grown up knowing one of her brothers—Will Herff. He'd stayed with his poor excuse for a father even after the lumber company was gone and the town was ruined by fire and flood.

Terrible circumstances had torn apart the Herff family, and

the one still suffering was Charlie, the middle child. Charlie had fixed himself in my heart when he was an abused, bullied, and brave boy of nine, rescuing me from the bad intentions of the Donnelly boys. He'd run away to escape their revenge, and only recently had come back to Winkler. Because his mind seemed damaged, we did not know who or what he remembered.

Glory had returned to Winkler to get to know Will, but she wasn't the only one in our circle who'd settled here because of him. According to Wanda, Virgie had taken up residence in one of his restored houses in hopes she'd have a chance to marry him. But Wanda got in her way, moving back at the same time with her daughter Evie, Glory and me. Then Barlow, bless him, had come looking for me.

"The kids'll be all right," Wanda said. "Things has always been that way." But not for Glory, who'd had the good fortune to grow up in Barlow's household in a proper town.

Most Saturday afternoons we brought our mending or knitting to Virgie's house and heard opinions about a more distant worry: the war in Europe. An avid collector of sensational news, Virgie insisted the war was not all that far away. "Soon every man and boy will be called up," she said. "I'd go myself, if they'd take me."

"They'd have to let you sew jewels on your soldier jacket," Glory said.

Virgie laughed and lifted her current project for our inspection, a brocade jacket on which she'd been sewing tiny gold beads of glass. Because she didn't attend church, Virgie wore her Sunday best at our Saturday gatherings. I would not be surprised if some Saturday she wore the beaded jacket.

We were all so used to each other that we could admire Virgie's fashions without feeling we had to keep up. Wanda's Aunt Piney always wore a long apron over her dress, and to us it didn't matter if it was starched and white or splattered by cooking and soiled by small muddy fingers. We were just glad when she could get away from the children and join us.

Virgie tended to squelch opposite opinions by talking faster and louder, so we usually let her have her say. There had already been two registrations for the draft, because the war department said men had not enlisted in sufficient numbers. In coal country, mothers and wives did not worry too much about the draft, because miners were deemed essential to the war effort and were usually given a Class Five draft status. Only a few young men from Winkler had chosen the army over a job in the mines.

"Mark my words," Virgie said, "if we don't stop the Kaiser over there in Europe, his soldiers will cross the ocean and burn our homes and kill us in terrible ways. They done it in Belgium, and now they're sinking so many of our ships we won't have any left to protect our shores."

I suspected that like the rest of us, Virgie had no vivid idea of our shores, but she used the word with patriotic feeling.

Thus far our greatest awareness of the war in Europe was the benefit to the coal economy in West Virginia and the rebuilding of our town. With coal needed to power trains, ships, and the manufacture of every kind of war material, four new mines had opened nearby, along with hastily-constructed houses for the influx of miners and their families.

"Every single one of us needs to keep an eye out for people who look like they don't belong," Virgie warned, "because those U-boats are dropping off spies in America right now. And if the Kaiser knows what's good for him, he'll cross these mountains and try to blow up our mines."

At this, we paused our needles and looked to see each other's reactions. We never wanted to believe Virgie, but she always managed to scare us a little.

CHAPTER 2

National threats were not as disturbing as our deepest, most personal fears, which we mostly kept to ourselves. In a mining town, everyone from operators to young children worried about dangers to the men, though Barlow said many operators feared more for their investment than for their workers' lives.

Barlow had two good partners, Randolph Bell, who served as mine engineer and superintendent, and Will, who kept busy as doctor for the miners and their families as well as for hill families who'd depended on him for years. The church, school and store, remnants of Winkler's lumbering days, belonged to Will, as well as the coal seam, which he contributed as his share of the partnership. The three had invested equally in the store goods and the miners' houses.

When we were first married, I'd walked with Barlow to his office each morning, passing women in doorways, their cheeks forced into smiles at the start of every shift that took their husbands into the black earth. Luzanna said a miner's wife never worried in ways that others could see or hear, for admitting the dangers would be like inviting them in.

Luzanna provided more insight to mining dangers than Barlow shared, because both John Donnelly and her second husband, Abner Hale, had worked in the mines. "Abner feared the gas," she said. "They carry safety lamps to warn of it, but a man can't keep an eye on the lamp all the time. That gas can creep along into small manways and kill with no more than a whiff. Then there's coal dust drifting everywhere. It'll catch with a spark and blow up the whole mine in a tornado of fire. Abner always said he'd rather die quick like that than be trapped behind a roof fall and have to eat his shoes till the air was gone. He never tried to put a brave face on the work like some do, but I got so I paid no heed to his muttering. In truth, times was always so bad that nothing mattered to me but feeding the kids. Men who work underground turn religious, don't you know. Or they drink, like John and Abner."

Barlow's role in the company did not require him to go underground, but he'd gone into the Winkler Mine at least once that he'd told me about. "I don't feel right about hiring men to go places I would not go myself," Barlow said.

I admired but feared his sentiment. "You're the best man to manage the company. There's no need to try your hand at blasting and shoveling coal."

"I'm sure I wouldn't be good at it, but I might adjust if I had to. It's blacker underground than you can imagine, blacker than night. A miner has no light but the glow of the lamp on his hat. And it's wet. Black and wet. Water seeps and drips and rats run everywhere. The roof timbers creak under the weight of a mountain overhead."

I'd heard enough.

WHEN ONLY A FEW OF US LIVED IN WINKLER, LUZANNA AND her children had felt free to open our door without invitation. In those days, Wanda, Evie and I lived together in one of Will's restored houses, and our front room was an improvised schoolroom. When we weren't having school, the children ran in and out with Evie. Since my marriage to Barlow and our move to the new house, even Wanda knocked and waited until she heard me say, "Please come in."

Such formality was a great loss. We'd laughed and cried so much together that my friends felt like family, and it seemed wrong for family to wait for an invitation. "It's only right to knock," Luzanna said. I knew why: she and the others were not as relaxed with Barlow. I had to accept that, though I kept saying, "Please, don't knock, just come in."

I said that to Alma when she tapped on my screen door one morning. She stood behind the screen, a girl with baby-smooth skin but all the other marks of a young woman. At sixteen, Alma Donnelly was perhaps at the summit of her beauty. Only she wasn't a Donnelly at all, and I don't know why I hadn't suspected it before. John Donnelly's mother had been round-faced, tall and broad with rusty brown hair, and her sons, John and Harry, had favored her. Luzanna's Emmy and Tim had round faces like them, and both looked like they'd soon be taller than their older sister, petite, black-haired Alma.

"Ma said I could talk to you," she said. "But I don't want to be a bother if you're busy."

"Not at all. Look, Freddy has stopped fussing. He's noticed there's a pretty girl in the room."

"Can I hold him?"

"Please do, it would be a help. Sit in the rocker. I'll take him back if he gets fussy, but while you've got him for the moment, I'll just run to the bathroom. It's hard for a mother to get time for things like that."

She was jiggling him on her lap and Freddy was laughing when I came back. "My, he loves you. But why shouldn't he? Everyone does."

She sighed. "I don't know where to start. Talking, I mean."

"Dear girl, I get lonely here. I'll gladly listen to anything you say."

"Some of this isn't nice. It has to do with boys and men."

"I'm acquainted with some of the faults of men. Have you talked with your ma?" I tried to keep my voice kind and steady, though I worried that Alma might be about to tell me a story of assault. I'd heard a lot of bad stories, but they were harder to take when they happened to someone I loved.

"I thought it might be easier to tell you before I told Ma. She said you'd be willing to talk about your first husband."

I settled in my easy chair. "Then I'll be the first to confide." I'd tried to forget that part of my life, but my mistakes might be useful to Alma. "His name was Jamie Long and I loved him at first sight. I had not yet turned eighteen."

"We'd stopped over in St. Louis—I was with my uncle and his daughters, on our way to the Dakota Territory. I've often wondered if I'd have married Jamie if I'd had a mother to advise me, or if my aunt had been alive. Everything might have been different. But maybe I wouldn't have listened."

"He was very handsome?"

"I thought so at the time, but he may have been no more handsome than any other man at that barn dance. I think it was his confidence. It made him stand out as someone superior. And when he cared to please, he was very gallant and entertaining. He sang while we danced, and his eyes sparkled when they looked into mine. His eyes were like Wanda's, mischievous, with the same thick lashes. Yes, I think he was beautiful. But I should not have given in to him for that alone. There was so much I didn't know."

"Like Wanda. Ma said you didn't know about her."

"Wanda turned out to the best thing I got from Jamie Long. But if I'd known about her in advance, I might not have been such a fool. When I found out about her, he claimed she wasn't his child, though it was plain to see."

My worst memories of Jamie did not feature him at all. I still turned cold and frantic, remembering the days and weeks when I'd been alone and snowed in. Of everything he did, neglect was the worst.

Alma helped Freddy stand on her lap. "So if a man hides the truth about himself, how can a girl keep from being fooled?"

"It may be easier if her parents know him and his family. To be fair, my uncle didn't like my choice, especially because Jamie thought he knew more than Uncle Bert about handling a horse team. Which we all clearly could see he did not. But if I'd been smart, I'd have rejected him on other grounds. First, he had no good words to say about his brother. That might have been all right, sometimes brothers don't get along, but he laughed when he told me about him, said Russell was stupid."

"That's Wanda's Uncle Russell?"

"That's right. Now Russell is different, but he's not stupid. I didn't know that for a long time. Jamie was contemptuous of many people, especially those who had more money. He said all rich men were crooks, but he wanted to be rich himself, and was sure he could make a fortune if he just got himself to the right place, like Texas or California."

"So a man should not make fun of people," she said, "or have big ideas of what he wants to do."

"I think it's all right to have aspirations. It's so hard to know, Alma. Even if he seems to be a good man in all respects, you may not be able to predict how he'll behave until you've been through hard times together. Then you see how he thinks and works, and if he helps when you're afraid."

"I may not know until I'm married?"

"Possibly true. Everyone says it's best to know a man several years before you marry. And to have some goals of your own."

"Like Miss Glory and Miss Virgie."

I nodded. "I understand how at a certain age, a girl thinks of boys all the time. And they want to be close to her, and many times she wants that too."

"The Bible says it's part of God's plan. Cleaving, being his woman."

"So it does. But I don't think the Bible always has the best advice for women. We're supposed to stand by and let our husbands decide our fate, but so often we're the ones who must carry the burdens and make the decisions."

Freddy began to squirm in Alma's arms, and I took him and let him nurse.

"Boys tease me," Alma said. "Last year in school they hung around in clumps, staring at me and talking behind their hands, and if there was no teacher in sight, blocking my way. They knew I didn't like it. And sometimes when I'm working in the store, a man bumps into me for no reason. Last year one touched me here." She pointed to her chest.

Startled, I sat straighter, interrupting Freddy's nursing. "Alma, sometimes boys tease because they don't understand what they're feeling and they don't know what else to do. But that business in the store? Your ma will be angry to hear it, as I am. You must tell Wanda, and tell her which men have bothered you. And where was Mr. Wise when this happened?" Wanda had given over management of the store to Mr. Wise, a recent hire. He always made a great show of efficiency and helpfulness in my presence, but Luzanna claimed he knew less than Alma.

"I don't like to tattle."

"Wanda needs to know. Mr. Wise doesn't bother you, does he?"

"He's always busy with the ladies. They laugh a lot when Wanda isn't there and the store isn't busy. I didn't tell anyone about those men because I was afraid Ma wouldn't let me work anymore. You know we need every cent."

"A good man would not try to touch you, and a good boy wouldn't talk about you to other boys."

"I don't want to be stuck up or mean, but I don't know how to be with boys. I'm afraid to be friendly, and I don't want most of them anywhere near me."

"It's safest to walk with your girlfriends. If you don't react when they tease you, they may laugh and call you cold and mean, but they may also be a little afraid of you."

"There was one boy I liked, but he joined the army. I think if I had a boyfriend or a husband those others would leave me alone."

Long ago I'd thought the same thing. "I wish that were true, but I'm afraid it isn't. Most would be respectful of your boyfriend or husband, but believe me, there are always a few who are looking to take advantage."

"So a girl is never safe?"

Freddy tired of nursing and I buttoned my dress. "I think we must always be aware."

CHAPTER 3

"**D**on't let on like you know," Luzanna said. "Alma wants to forget about it."

Everyone in our circle understood. It wasn't the girl's fault that a man had touched a private part of her body. Even a mature woman would be embarrassed. Wanda's Aunt Piney was red-faced, just hearing of it.

"I'd have slapped him silly," Virgie said. "The dirty old thing."

That day Wanda had brought Otis to our gathering and Piney had brought Ralphie, her husband's youngest grandchild. The two little boys had been sitting on Virgie's parlor floor, stacking empty thread spools and knocking them down. Ralphie now grabbed Piney's ball of twisted wool and began to wrap it around her.

Wanda got up, set Ralphie firmly on a chair, and freed her aunt. "The old coot got worse than a slap—Will fired him. And when Alma showed me the others that bothered her, I told them to stay out of the store. They can let their women buy their tobacco."

Distant squeals and shouts gave us a moment's pause. Glory stood and looked through the screen door. "It's just boys playing in the river."

Otis perked up and ran to the door and Ralphie slipped from his chair. Glory stopped their escape by slipping the screen door's latch into its eye. The little boys pressed their hands and foreheads to the screen.

"A mother has to get used to a lot of dangers," Luzanna said. "You do what you can to protect your kids, then you have to stop thinking."

৩৯৩

SOON WE WERE ALL THINKING AND WORRYING ABOUT WANDA.

Even the smallest, nicest towns seemed to have their share of scandal, and that summer a nasty rumor forced me into confrontation with my stepdaughter. It was first whispered to me by her Aunt Piney.

"This ain't nice, but I been holding it in for a week," Piney said, "and I've gotta tell someone. It's about Wanda and that teacher." Piney was a soft-spoken, timid woman, and this subject caused her eyes to blink rapidly and her voice to tremble. "He's the one that sings so fine in church. I can't bring myself to talk to her about it, but I thought maybe you could."

If a rumor was going around about Wanda and a man other than her husband, I didn't have to ask what kind. "She goes to his house almost every night," Piney said.

I could not believe Wanda would be untrue to Will, but I knew better than anyone that she was not predictable. I promised to talk with her. It had to be nothing, for anything else would hurt like death. From that moment, I had a new worry.

The next Saturday I got my opportunity to speak to Wanda about the rumors. She came to my house before our gathering with a stack of her boy's outgrown clothes, and we walked together to Virgie's.

Our house sat alone on the highest street, where Will and Randolph intended to build their homes someday. Below us stretched long rows of new company houses, smaller and of unpainted wood. Virgie's home was two streets down, one of six houses left from Winkler's days as a busy lumber town.

Since Piney's visit I'd suffered quietly about the rumors surrounding my stepdaughter, and I was nervous about confronting her. Believing the best way to say something difficult was to say it quickly, I came right out with it as soon as we turned toward Virgie's.

"Wanda, there's gossip about you and a teacher. I thought you should know."

She laughed. "About me and Grady Malone? Well talk's cheap. Forget it, Ma. It don't matter 'cause it ain't true."

I expected that kind of answer, but I wasn't sure she meant it. "People can still be hurt," I said.

"I'm fine."

"You're fine, but what about Will? And Evie? She's old enough to understand, and her friends may be talking."

Wanda had always been contemptuous of society's rules, though since marrying Will she had tried to tame her bushy hair into a bun like everyone else, and in cold weather she wore a petticoat under her skirt instead of men's trousers.

"Evie will believe what I tell her. And I've told Will it's nothing but singing. He's wrong not to trust me. Now you too?"

I was sad to hear the singing practice had become an argument between her and Will. When we turned up the steps to Virgie's house, I said, "I trust you, and I'm sure Will trusts you. It's how it looks, a woman and man spending nearly every evening together."

"Not spending, Ma, practicing. I don't want that man. I just want to sing with him."

"Please give this some thought. Evie may be teased at school —you know what that's like. And you can't disregard Will's feelings."

"Will is out lots of nights, seeing all sorts of women."

"His patients," I said.

"That's right, Ma. Nobody thinks that's scandalous, no matter if he sees what's under a woman's vest and bloomers. He's following his calling. And singing's my calling. I buried it all these years, but Grady's brought it back. I'm singing with Grady, not lifting my skirt."

Wanda walked ahead into Virgie's parlor, greeting everyone not with "hello" but with a continuation of her argument. "Will don't understand how I need to sing. It's only an hour in the evenings. I'm not gonna stop."

The four other women in Virgie's parlor abruptly stopped their needlework and stared as though they'd heard a rumble in the earth. At that moment I realized my friends and I depended not only on mutual aid and shared events but also on the assurance that we knew everything about each other. Since it was true for me it must also be true of the others: each of us kept portions of ourselves secret, with the possible exception of Glory, who seemed too young to have experienced anything worth hiding.

Like Virgie, Wanda could be embarrassingly frank, so we believed she always told the truth as she understood it. But until now, none of us had revealed sharp disagreements with our husbands or children, for that would be disloyal. Confessing a dispute in her marriage threatened the certainty that behind our closed doors all was well. Our friends looked dismayed to learn she would do nothing to stop the gossip.

She faced us with hands on hips. "So how do I make him understand?"

"Understand about Grady? He won't never," Virgie said. "And you wouldn't neither."

Glory looked down at her knitting and began to pull out a row. Beside her, Luzanna lifted a needle to thread it in better light. Glory might say something privately to Wanda later, but I did not expect Luzanna to reveal whatever she might be thinking. Nor would Wanda's Aunt Piney, who was nervous in the presence of an argument and shy about giving advice.

Virgie raised her eyebrows and smiled wickedly. "Watch out, Wanda. You're not the onliest one that came back to Winkler to get Will Herff. I would've had him if you hadn't butted in."

"Please," Piney said.

Wanda said, "Please what?"

Piney looked startled. She opened her mouth, then closed it and lowered her eyes.

"I'm never alone with Grady! The piano player is there."

"Also a man," Virgie said.

"Well Virgie, if it was you and two men I'd worry for *their* reputations."

Everyone laughed but Wanda, who turned her back on the others. "Ma, I gotta have this. Talk to Will. He thinks you walk on water." She sounded like a child coaxing to get her way.

"Wanda, I can't. Not this time."

"You want me to give up what I want."

"No, I want both you and Will to be happy." I was saddened at that moment by how much she looked like her father, who had never cared about anyone's happiness but his own.

CHAPTER 4

Since the opening of our mine, Winkler had grown from six houses to hundreds built for workers and their families. The town had electricity again, and a lucky few had flush toilets and hot water boilers. That summer motorized vehicles reached us on a hard-paved road from the north. Along with horses and wagons, the new vehicles sometimes created confusion on Main Street, giving us the sense that Winkler was catching up with modern towns. But prosperity always comes at a price. Here that meant dangerous work, smoke and rumbling of trains, shift whistles, and the steady beat of ventilation fans. And though Barlow and I were cramped into two rooms, I couldn't deny that we were putting money in the bank because our employees were poor. The Coal Operators' Protective Association had stuck them with a miserable wage. Barlow said there was nothing he and his partners could do about it.

The summer's steamy nights raised resentments and inflamed both Freddy's diaper rash and my husband's concern about tensions between owners and workers. Even though Randolph was dedicated to mine safety and Will seemed to care more for the people's welfare than for the price of coal, the guarded glances of the wives said they knew we were the same as owners everywhere.

We'd made no friends among the town's new residents, a fact that Barlow said might be for the best—it would be hard to fire a man if he knew the names of his children. And though our miners seemed glad to have their new jobs and homes, we feared their satisfaction would not last long. Even people with no family in the mines knew enough about the mine wars at Paint Creek to fear the consequences of a confrontation between workers pushed to their limits and owners with guns and government on their side.

None of us had been to Paint Creek but we knew it was somewhere in the southern part of our state. Miners there had gone out on strike just six years ago and battled guards and federal troops for more than a year while their families lived through the winter in tents. My friends and I had no personal experience of the hard-heartedness that caused men to shoot at each other, yet we'd heard enough to believe the stories from that time.

Members of our Coal Operators' Association believed that owners of mines along Paint Creek had rightly protected their property, but Barlow and his partners thought their methods had created the disaster. They'd hired guards from the Baldwin-Felts Detective Agency to turn striking miners out of their company houses. Though we'd heard conflicting reports, most agreed the greatest atrocity had occurred when guards fired machine guns into tent camps and houses from the safety of an armored train. When at last the strike was settled, much had been lost and little gained. I tried not to wonder what Barlow and I might do in such a situation.

The women in my circle didn't talk about a repetition of Paint Creek occurring here, but everyone knew it was possible. For now, we lived in peace. While our country was engaged in the war in Europe, miners everywhere had pledged to work even harder and not to strike.

"The preacher was at it again," Barlow said, the next day after church. "Today he told the congregation how lucky they are to be exempt from the draft, do vital work and live in a safe place with all the coal they need, because the Fuel Administration has ordered everyone else in the country to cut back."

Freddy had finally gone down for his nap, so my arms and hands were free to help Barlow off with his suit coat. His collar was wet and his damp shirt stuck to his back. Because I hadn't been to church since Freddy turned colicky, I hadn't heard the new preacher, jointly hired and supported by our mine and two others nearby. Wanda said most Sundays he yelled the same damning text, but attendance was good because church was the best excuse to do nothing but sit, and before the service folks could gossip and show off anything new, like babies. I hoped to return and show off Freddy someday.

"He manages to use the operators' favorite scripture in every sermon," Barlow said. "Blessed are the poor!"

In my short term as an owner's wife, I'd come to hate the Coal Operators' Protective Association, made up of thirty owners and some seventy mines, the most distant an hour by train. At the start of the war, the operators had agreed to raise wages from 22 to 25 cents a ton, which meant a man who blasted and loaded coal might earn three to five dollars a day, depending on his strength and stamina. In return for three cents more on a ton, the miners had accepted the Fuel Administration's directive not to strike during the war. Barlow said the men were patriotic, but every miner in our region knew that union mines in the northern counties paid 60 cents a ton. Those mines, however, weren't currently hiring, and their miners were not fully employed because non-union coal was cheaper.

Barlow regularly came home from church as agitated as he returned from association meetings. "This preacher is no more than a mouthpiece for the association," he said. "I'd like our families to hear someone better. Hell, I'd like to hear someone better, too. He's so condescending to the operators, it's embarrassing."

"You could stop attending," I said. "Or go to the Catholic service. Would anyone notice? Or care?"

"Either solution might be better than hating Sunday. Thank goodness I can come home to you." He loosened his tie. "How was Freddy this morning?"

"Better." The baby had been his usual cranky self, but Barlow did not need to hear my troubles. "I don't want you to hate Sundays, or any day." As I unhooked his tight collar button, I caressed his neck with one finger, then pressed my face against his shirt front. In some ways we were still shy with each other. Perhaps because of our past, he often approached me as though afraid I might push him away. I tried to make up for that with encouraging touches. We'd had few loving moments since Freddy had seized control of my life.

"I'm sorry I'm always busy with the baby, such a nervous mother."

"That boy is probably as difficult to live with as I am. But you..." He surprised me with a hard kiss. "Are perfect."

I preferred he know my faults and love me anyway. "I am not perfect. If I hadn't been so stubborn back then, we might now have six tall children. And years together."

"Ah, girl. Come and help me off with these hot clothes."

Hand in hand we stepped quietly into the darkened room where Freddy was sleeping. The room was crowded with our bed, the baby crib, our clothes press, cedar chests and the fainting couch Barlow had given me as a wedding present.

At this moment I did not want to think of Freddy, so I did not look to see if he was awake, but laid our clothes on the fainting couch and turned down the bedspread. When we drew close on the cool sheet I knew how starved my skin had been for his, and his for mine.

With unusual mercy, Freddy slept on, and after we returned to the kitchen and enjoyed dinner without a crying baby, I was certain everything would get better.

SINCE FREDDY'S BIRTH, WANDA HAD STOPPED BY TO CHECK ON us almost every day, and when the next week went by with no visits, I told myself she only needed time to work things out with her husband. Even so, the sudden change in our old routine added another layer of worry to my hours alone. Luzanna's visits saved me. The best person to help another through anxious times was someone who knew them well.

"It wasn't easy, but I told Alma about her real pa," Luzanna said. "It didn't hurt me none and I don't think it surprised her a lot. For sure I've earned no respect, the way I've lived. She knows me and Abner Hale was never legal-married."

"Your children love you, and you've done better than a lot of men, keeping them fed and clothed."

"Not always. But you helped us rise, you and Wanda, Will and the others."

"We've all been down and out, Luzanna. Barlow's sister rescued Wanda and me when we needed a place to stay. I'll never forget that."

In the way of every woman who knew about hard times, Luzanna did not probe for particulars. "We have to make the best," she said. "And we must pass what we know to our girls. Alma said she don't mind the boys' teasing so much since you talked to her. And I'm glad you made her tell Wanda about those men in the store."

NEITHER WANDA NOR PINEY WAS PRESENT WHEN I ARRIVED AT Virgie's house the next Saturday. That afternoon we were helping Luzanna make gloves to sell at the August Trading Days. Will had started the market when he was Winkler's only resident. It was always held on the weekend nearest the full moon, and filled the town with buyers and sellers from nearby towns and mountain farms.

When Piney arrived, Glory was tracing patterns on a soft deerskin, while I cut, Virgie punched holes for the needle, and Luzanna stitched. "I can't stay," Piney said. She was breathing hard and had spots of red on her plump cheeks and forehead.

"Sit for a minute," Virgie ordered.

Piney dropped into the nearest chair. "It's Blanche. She's back."

"Well knock me over," Virgie said. "I thought this time she was gone for good."

"I'm sorry," I said. We all knew about Simpson's daughter, the mother of his three grandchildren, and we knew the part she'd played when her husband Raz and his brother Coyne Cotton had kidnapped Wanda. Out of respect for Simpson, we kept Blanche's role to ourselves. Piney said he didn't know, because of course Blanche didn't think she'd done anything wrong since a wife was duty-bound to help her husband.

Virgie brought Piney a glass of water. "Drink that. Simpson should bar the door. Blanche has been gone what, most of three years?"

I feared the same thing Piney must be thinking, that Blanche would try to take away the three children she'd left with her father and Piney. "Did she come alone?"

"She says she did, but who knows? She come yesterday on the train. Ruby is the only one of the kids who remembers her." Piney sniffed. "And I think Ruby's afraid her father will come back too, even though we told her he's dead. Simpson says he beat Blanche, and we think he beat Ruby too. I gotta get home.

Blanche is trying to make up with the kids, and they don't like it."

"Come and get me if she tries to leave with them kids," Virgie said. "If Simpson won't stand up to her, I'll set her straight."

"Oh, Virgie," Piney said. "I don't think that'll be necessary."

"Don't bet on it," Virgie said. "I knowed Blanche a long time —she was a sweet and simple girl, but she's never had no judgment, and she learned bad ways when she married that Raz Cotton. It's a good thing he's gone." Virgie turned to Glory, the only one of us who might not know that story. "Piney's ma killed him."

"Lucie Bosell killed Blanche's husband? Really?" Glory slid into the chair beside Piney and took her hand. "Was he hurting one of the children?"

Virgie favored the most dramatic interpretation of events, and usually I took her stories with a grain of salt. "Lucie didn't kill him," I said. "Raz fell backwards down the store steps." I hadn't lived in Winkler at the time, but I believed the story as Will and Wanda had told it.

Virgie shrugged. "I guess that's one side of the truth. But he fell because Lucie was shooting at him. Stumbled and fell and cracked his head open, which he wouldn't of done but for her."

"He was robbing the store," Piney said. "Him and his brother Coyne. They was after guns, and Ma and Ruth was in there alone, staying in one of Will's rooms. I was living with Simpson and the kids at the time, and the town was full of campers here for a stock sale."

"I saw him spread out dead on them steps," Virgie said. "Me and Wanda was in a meeting at my house with the sheriff and some others, trying to figure how to get the goods on Raz and Coyne for kidnapping and all. So we got there right after. It's a wonder Lucie didn't shoot us too. The store was all dark, and when she heard someone breaking in, Lucie shot it up. You know she's half blind."

Piney handed the water glass to Virgie. "I gotta get back."

We resumed our work with gloomy faces. "I feel bad for Piney," Luzanna said. "She doesn't deserve this."

We didn't speak of it, but Piney always seemed helpless against anyone ready to take advantage.

"After Raz died, Blanche took up with the first man who'd have her," Virgie said. "Whenever a man tosses her out, she remembers she left the kids with her father. She was always kinda dim, but oh so pretty. Maybe her looks have changed. Maybe that's why she's back."

Glory held a pattern down with one hand and traced an outline on deerskin with chalk. "What happened to her husband's brother?"

"There was three," Virgie said. "Coyne, the oldest, got away. The youngest was Duck and he got stabbed to death behind the church one night during Trading Days. It was the same summer but earlier."

"What a family," Glory said.

Maybe it wasn't a good idea, but we'd tried to keep Glory from knowledge of her father, especially since Will seemed determined not to disparage him. We'd told her of her father's carving skills but not of his bad temper. Unless she asked, I wasn't going to tell her he'd been killed in a brawl, though it was possible Will had done so. I didn't know about Virgie's family, but it seemed like all of us had at least one disreputable ancestor. My father had left me with his sister when my mother died, and we'd never heard of him again.

"Piney and Simpson are lucky to have each other," I said. "And it might be good if those kids could take the name Wainwright instead of having to be known as Cottons."

"Piney was a lifesaver for Simpson when Blanche dropped off those kids," Virgie said. "Him, me and Will was the only ones living in the whole town, and Simpson was building his gristmill.

There was no way he could take care of them, him being alone, the middle one hard to handle and Ralphie just a baby. But I don't think Piney will be bothered with Blanche for long. If she ain't lost her looks, she'll get another man and be off. Meanwhile, it might be best if she don't run into Wanda."

CHAPTER 5

Much as I liked Will, I was not overly glad when he came to our back porch the next afternoon, because the look on his face made me certain he'd come to talk about Wanda. I didn't want to choose sides, and I had no idea how I could help.

"You go on," Barlow said, after Will said he needed a private word. Barlow took Freddy from my arms and sat on the porch rocker.

Will and I moved a few steps away to our table in the yard. "It's Wanda," he said.

"Yes?" I took a deep breath and prepared for a difficult conversation.

"You know she goes to that man's house almost every night. Everybody knows."

"We've talked about it," I said.

"Wanda doesn't care what other people think as long as she's right in her own mind. She says it's not about him, and I think she means it. But I'm not sure of that man's intentions. And it's not right, her going off and leaving Otis with Evie when I'm called out at night. One of us should be at home."

By now Will must know that living with Wanda would never be easy. "Have you met the teacher?" I'd believed her when she said her purpose was no more than singing. It hadn't occurred to me that the teacher's intentions might be different.

"I wasn't present when the school board interviewed him, but I've heard him sing in church. I suppose when school begins he'll have less time for evenings with my wife. What if I talked with him? Would that be too low?"

"Wanda can be heedless of danger," I said, "especially when there's something she wants. She stopped singing after her ma died. Before that I think she sang to lift her mind from everything bad. And you remember she had a lot to forget. Then she met Homer, and he was all she wanted, and after he died she met you again, and you were all she wanted."

"But now..."

"She's devoted to you and the children. But presently she seems inspired." I hesitated, then said the words that had been floating in my mind. "As you were inspired when you went away to study medicine. For an entire year."

"Wanda and I weren't married then."

"It was a dark time. We had very little to sustain us here, and she was expecting a child."

"And never said!"

"Will, I'm not accusing you. She thought going away meant you didn't care for her. She also knew that being a good doctor was important to you."

He shook his head. "I know I work too much. I got used to that when I was here alone, but now I'd be happy to be home with my family. So would everyone. Look at the miners. Everyone sacrifices for the ones they love."

"And your wife would go down in the mine and do the dirtiest, most dangerous job if it was the only way to take care of you and the children, but she doesn't have to do that. She's a lot like you and Glory: you have many gifts, and you want to use them all."

"Do you think it's good for her to...practice every night?"

"I've told her I do not, and our friends say the same thing."

"I know she loves to sing. I don't want to take that away," Will said.

"You couldn't go with her?"

"It's not possible. Every night I'm called out to see someone sick, or I've got an association or school board meeting."

"It might be better if the teacher came to your home. If you had a piano, you could invite people for an evening of music as we used to do in the boardinghouse. Everyone needs something beyond work."

"You're right, of course. I could get a piano, but we don't have a proper place to put it or to entertain people." He paused like he was thinking. "I know we shouldn't be living in the store. It's convenient, and at present there's no empty house. Maybe she'd be content to stay at home if she had a real one."

I didn't think Wanda cared where she lived, but I'd heard jealousy when she spoke of Will's female patients. "She might be more content if she could work with you. You could ask her to assist with your patients."

"Assist? What could she do?"

"Whatever you wanted to teach her." I hoped I was right.

"I'll try anything," he said. "I didn't think being married would be so hard."

"I know."

He smiled toward the porch where Barlow was bouncing Freddy on his knee. "I want the two of us to be like you."

I smiled too, because looking at my husband always made me feel better. "We made our mistakes," I said.

"I've thought about firing that teacher. I could do it today, get him out of town like Barlow and the sheriff got rid of the Donnellys, do you remember? But that would be wrong, wouldn't it?"

"I don't think it would be wise." Like throwing fuel on a fire.

IN THE WEEKS AFTER BLANCHE INSERTED HERSELF BACK INTO her father's house, Piney did not attend our gatherings. Luzanna guessed she was wearing herself out, taking care of everybody in the house, which now included her husband's daughter.

"I stop by every day or so," Virgie said, "just so Blanche knows I'm paying attention."

Hearing the children had measles, I'd stayed away, but I'd given fresh beef and potatoes for meals that Luzanna cooked and delivered.

I also hadn't seen Wanda since we'd argued about her visits to Grady Malone's house. When I came home from Virgie's one Saturday, Barlow said I should make the first move. "Wanda's been faithful about coming here while you've confined yourself to home. Put Freddy in the buggy and pay her a visit."

I hadn't confided even to Barlow how the baby's crying made me ashamed to take him in public. I had other reasons for keeping him home—fear he'd bother others, and the fact that when he fussed I couldn't give my attention to anything else.

When I hesitated, Barlow said, "Go on, I'll stay here with Freddy."

"Are you sure?" I didn't want my husband to resent me or be sorry we had a child with needs I couldn't satisfy.

"We'll be fine. Come back before dark."

When I reached the store, Wanda and Will were mounting their horses, and Will had his doctor bag tied to his saddle. Evie sat with Otis on the store steps.

"It's good you come, for I was going to ride up to get you," Wanda said. "Aunt Ruth's in a bad way—Price Loughrie rode in to fetch Will. I need you take Otis and Evie till I get back, maybe a few days. Evie's good about minding Otis, but I don't like to leave them overnight."

"Of course. Is there anything else I can do?"

Will turned his horse. "People with an emergency should call on Dr. Pringle in Barbara Town. Would you letter a sign for my door?"

"Here comes Price," Wanda said. "He went to change his horse for one of Uncle Russell's."

"I hope you'll find Ruth doing better," I said.

Price Loughrie did not come to greet me in his usual gentlemanly way, but raised his hat and put his horse into a trot. Daylight would soon be gone, and Wanda's aunt and granny lived several hours away.

"Otis, be a good boy," Wanda called. "Evie, get his stroller."

We watched them ride down the street. Where in our two rooms, I wondered, would I put two more children? "This will be like old times," I said, turning to Evie. "I never see enough of you." She was a dutiful girl, going on fourteen and a joy to be with, but her little brother was another story. "Let's go inside and make that sign for the doctor's door, and you can gather up what you'd like to take."

"Where will I sleep?"

"Oh, we have lots and lots of room. We'll explore the rest of the house and you can choose." Evie was familiar with the unfinished rooms of our house where Luzanna and I hung the wash on rainy or snowy days, with its boarded-up window spaces, missing doors, and sawdust on bare wood floors. At least the rooms had the nice scent of new wood, and each had an electric bulb suspended from a ceiling fixture.

"We'll set up one of the new beds in a front room downstairs," I said. Barlow and I had returned from our wedding trip with wagons of crated furniture, most of it still boxed in rooms with unhung windows and stacks of unvarnished trim. I'd begun to think we would always live this way, for with men at war and a shortage of labor everywhere, he'd found no available builder other than himself and Simpson for a few hours here and there. Barlow's partners were no better off; Will, Wanda, Otis and Evie living in rooms in the store, and Randolph in one of the company houses with very little furniture, according to Luzanna, who cooked for him and did his laundry.

On our walk home, Otis insisted on helping Evie push his new metal stroller, but when we turned uphill, he decided he should ride. We turned the stroller around and pulled it backwards up the steepest parts, because Otis was big and heavy for his age.

"Ma said we should tell Aunt Piney," Evie said, when we neared the turn to Piney's house.

"You go ahead, but don't go inside. Nobody's said if the kids are over the measles."

"Oh, Granny, Aunt Piney's gonna cry. Would you do it?"

Evie and Otis waited at the intersection to Piney's street. Simpson sat on his porch, playing checkers with Ruby, his oldest grandchild, now seven. He was a strong man and a good provider, but today his cheeks sagged and his eyes looked tired. From inside came mixed sounds from a crying child and a woman singing.

"Ruth is sick," I said, "and Wanda's gone to the farm. Shall I tell Piney, or would it be better if you did it, maybe at another time?"

Simpson closed his eyes for a moment. "When Piney hears it, she'll want to go right away, and Robert's still sick, and Blanche..."

"I understand. Tell Piney she should wait until Wanda comes back. If she needs to go then, we'll think of something." I ended by saying he could send Ruby and the youngest to me the next day. "I'll give them lunch and we'll play school."

"Piney needs a spot of rest," he said. "I'm in your debt."

"Simpson, Barlow and I are always in your debt."

In the space of an hour I'd agreed to take care of four additional children, though I felt inadequate to manage one. The brightening in Simpson's face made me determined to accept disruption as normal. If I could do that, everything might be easier.

CHAPTER 6

B efore Piney had an opportunity to go to the farm, Ruth Bosell died. She had been weak for some time with an ailment we did not talk about, though she was widely known as a heavy drinker. Once again I left Freddy in his father's care so I could attend Ruth's funeral. I cried through most of the service, not for Wanda, who sang "Near to the Heart of God" and "Church in the Wildwood," nor for Ruth's mother, Lucie Bosell, but for Piney, Ruth's sister. She and Simpson sat in the front row with his grandchildren. That day all three behaved well, sneaking frightened faces at their sobbing Granny Piney.

Price Loughrie did not attend the funeral. Occasional preacher, one-time marshal and rumored bootlegger, Price was Ruth's close companion in drink, who constantly tried to reform her as well as himself. I was disappointed that he'd found some reason not to attend. Barlow considered him a friend, and I liked to hear him play the violin, which he managed very well even when he couldn't walk straight.

When I expressed my sympathy, Wanda said, "I don't know what we're gonna do about Granny. Price has flown the coop, and I don't think she can get along on the farm by herself."

Half the mourners at the funeral might have come just to get a look at Wanda's granny, the infamous Lucie Bosell, who according to legend had made illegal whiskey and murdered a revenue man. We knew the whiskey part was true. The old woman was deaf and half blind, and she gave the audience more fuel for new gossip, repeating loudly throughout the service that the preacher was going on too long, it was hot, and nobody had come to get saved.

After the funeral, Piney announced that she and the children were going to go to the farm and stay with her ma until Simpson located Loughrie, or Lucie agreed to move to town. We were standing on the street in front of the church with Luzanna, Virgie and Glory.

Virgie put forth the question troubling my mind. "And what about Blanche?"

"We're gonna sneak away early tomorrow. Half the time Blanche don't seem to know them kids. It might be a whole day before she figures out we're gone—she always sleeps late. Then she won't find us without someone showing the way. Even if she does, Ma will likely scare her off."

🐚🔖

FOR ME, LIFE GOT BETTER BEFORE IT GOT WORSE. SEPTEMBER 6 of 1918, Frederick Barlow Townsend turned six months old, began to crawl, and overnight it seemed, outgrew his colic. And finally, Wanda visited my house again, bringing Evie and Otis.

"I can't stay long," Wanda said. "Today I've got to train two new clerks, one to take my place and one for Alma's. She thinks she should get one more year of high school."

"We're getting a piano," Evie said. "I'm going to have lessons. Ma too."

"I'm not gonna stop singing," Wanda said, "but I won't have much time for it, 'cause I'll be making house calls with Will."

Wanda was always eager for something new, but today she

looked excited. Another one of my worries faded away. "I'm happy for both you and Will. You'll make a fine assistant."

"For sure I ain't afraid of blood or puke or shit," she said, smiling as Otis gave a hard tug to my skirt. "I could probably work in the slaughterhouse with Uncle Russell." She pulled a white cloth cap from her dress pocket. "Will got this for me, and a white apron too. Good thing about the cap is it holds my hair from falling down." She tucked her hair under its edges. "What do you think?"

I lifted Otis to my lap. "Very smart," I said.

"It's not smart, it looks like a granny cap, but it don't matter. Anyway, I've come to ask if you'll keep Otis half a day. He gives everybody trouble but you and me and Evie. She's been minding him, but school starts tomorrow. I don't know why Alma thinks she needs to go—she probably knows more than the teacher. I said maybe the store could pay her more, but no, she wants that schooling."

"Alma loves to learn," I said. Glad as I was to hear of these changes for Wanda, I was reluctant to take Otis. I'd kept him when she started working in the store, but that was before Freddy's birth, and Otis now seemed as heedless of instruction as his mother.

I loosened Otis's hug on my neck, keeping my eyes on Freddy, who was sitting on a folded quilt near our feet. For his sake as well as for my husband's, I needed to be stronger against Wanda's plans for me. "You know I love your boy, but I've so much to catch up on here."

"I'll bring the baby pen that Will made," she said. "It will be good for Freddy and you can stick Otis in it too when you have to tend to other things. Half a day, Ma, just until the school day ends. Then Evie will come for him."

"Wherever will I put a baby pen?" Our kitchen was a spacious room with an iron and enamel stove, a deep granite sink, a pie safe, and a flower-patterned linoleum floor, but with the other rooms unfinished, we'd crowded it by adding a hassock and two sitting room chairs.

Naturally she had a solution. "You got three work tables in here—move some of them out."

I set Otis on his feet in order to grab up Freddy, who was crawling off his quilt onto a floor that seemed impossible to keep clean. Unhappy to be put down, Otis whined and tugged on Freddy's leg, catching me off guard and pulling the baby from my grasp. I caught him just before his head would have hit the floor. Freddy wailed, and Otis puckered up and cried too.

Wanda laughed. "Otis is jealous, but you watch, they'll be great buddies."

With so much at stake for Wanda and Will, I couldn't say no.

SINCE THIS WAS TO BE MY LAST DAY WITH ONLY ONE CHILD, that afternoon I put on my second-best dress and wheeled Freddy out of the house in his new wicker buggy. If we saw Barlow, he would be happy that I was finally using the buggy he'd ordered as soon as we knew a baby was on the way. And perhaps this would be the day I began to make friends among the other women in town. One exchange of names and a short conversation would be a satisfactory start.

My friends assumed the miners' wives had started the rumors about Wanda and the singer. But we'd never know, because the wives did not confide in us. They always greeted me by name, but for me there were too many new names to learn and no good opportunities to learn them. Any time I tried to start a conversation with a woman I didn't know, she acted like a pupil being asked to recite or a thief required to account for herself. In the Methodist Church, the wives had started a Ladies' Aid Society, but they gave no open invitation, and none in my circle had been approached to join. "Don't bother with them," Virgie had said. "They think we're snobs, but they're the ones that are picky about who can be a friend and who can't."

"They're not even friendly to me," Luzanna said.

Virgie maintained it was their loss. "I've not a doubt they'd like you if you wasn't friends with May Rose and Wanda. Who knows? They might like me too."

"You'd have to stop smiling at their husbands," Wanda said. "You can bet they gossip about every one of us 'cause we're the ones they don't know much about. But especially me, account of how they like my husband. You should see the way they line up in his waiting room with their kids' runny noses and their female complaints."

"I've seen you smiling at their husbands while you sell tobacco and such," Virgie said. "And at Trading Days? Wanda, you're as forward as me."

Wanda shrugged. "You gotta be accommodating to sell."

"It's one thing to be nice," Luzanna said, "but I tell Alma never to stare into no man's eyes. That's asking for trouble."

"She'll have to do it someday, 'less she wants to be an old maid," Virgie said. "I still don't know how May Rose knew Barlow was interested, seeing how she avoided looking at him most of the time."

As usual, this kind of talk went on and on. I wondered if Wanda had smiled too much at Grady Malone, and if she was still doing it. As so often happened, our talk that day had veered to a discussion of men and the qualities of a good one. I suppose that was a kind of gossip, though until we confronted Wanda about the teacher, we'd never spoken of any man in particular. I wished it wasn't so, but I feared we'd be speaking of him again.

I'd never taken the buggy out by myself, and now as I walked downhill, holding it back, I realized the return trip would be harder. But Freddy was sitting up and looking about with his dimpled hands clutching the sides, enjoying the sunshine as much as I. He'd had no lengthy tantrums for two days, and I was not going to risk one now by taking him back to the house.

At the first cross street I looked automatically toward Piney and Simpson's house. I was eager for Piney to see Freddy so transformed, his face smiling and pink instead of scrunched and red, but she and the children were still at the farm with Lucie Bosell. Wanda said living with Lucie would be no easier for Piney than living with Blanche.

A young woman approached from a side street, and I stopped the buggy to greet her. She carried a baby older than mine, had one toddler hanging onto her skirt and another following behind, scooting his feet in the dust. "Good morning." She bobbed her head. "That's a pretty dress."

I thanked her. "My friends made it for me, a wedding present." The dress was faded from the wash but still my favorite, ankle length with a dropped waist and broad white collar. Glory had bought the material, Virgie had made the pattern, and Luzanna had done most of the needlework.

"It heartens me to hear talk of good friends," the woman said. "There's no kindlier folk than the poor, 'cause at times each other is all we got, don't you think?"

"Indeed." I admired her cheery attitude, but wondered if she'd been ill. Bony ridges surrounded her deep-set eyes, and her hands were red and cracked. Her voice sounded young, but her mouth and cheeks were drawn in.

"I ain't made any friends yet but we ain't been here long, and I been busy."

"I'm very glad to meet you. My name is May Rose."

She looked away to the child who had let go of her skirt and now sat swirling his hands in the dust. "Mine's Etta Karakas."

The other child came forward, gripped the edges of the buggy and rocked it. Freddy laughed, and I lifted him and held him close. The Karakas child had a runny nose.

"I'm going to the store," I said. "Shall we walk together?"

"Thank you kindly, but I'm off to work."

"To work? With the children?"

"They do fine. I clean up the roadhouse." She gave a nervous laugh. "They're slow walkers, though."

Everyone knew about the roadhouse a mile north of town, a place that looked like an ordinary dwelling but had a back entrance to a speak-easy basement. One of the mine operators was rumored to own it. Some said he controlled how much scrip the bartender could let workers from that mine spend on drink. Barlow said for a lot of men, the thought of a drink after work was the only thing that helped them endure the dark perils of their shift.

A mile seemed a long way for Mrs. Karakas's little ones to walk. She shifted the child in her arms, pulled one up from the dust, and urged the other away from the buggy.

I watched her go, thinking I should offer Freddy's buggy, but it felt wrong to give away his father's gift. Simpson had made a wagon for his grandchildren; perhaps I could get him to make one for Mrs. Karakas. And I would ask Luzanna if she knew why the woman had to work, if her husband was injured or sick or if he drank his wages at the roadhouse.

I encountered other women as I pushed the buggy along Main Street. They kept their distance, but a few of their children ran up to see Freddy. They were called back, warned not to bother Mrs. Townsend.

To me the women's rigid faces signaled their discontent, though I thought they must know they were better off than women whose husbands worked for other association mines. Other operators had raised the price of goods in their company stores, effectively wiping out the three-cent pay increase the miners had received at the start of the war. The Winkler store hadn't raised prices, but I hadn't heard of anyone thanking us.

I'd asked Barlow why the wages of our miners had to be controlled by the association. He'd said the Winkler Mine was free to leave the association, but then we might suddenly have no way to ship our coal, because the railroad company owned the most mines and controlled the association. "For the time being, the only thing we can do is make our mine a safer and better place to work and our town a good place to live," he said.

I wished the miners and their families would see that my husband and his partners were trying to be fair. I tried not to resent them.

Freddy looked left and right, gurgling at the children and turning his head to see everything on the industrial side of the street, which was lined with coal cars and docks of mine supplies. His delight made me certain I'd kept him too much in the house, restricting his awareness of the world.

Two buildings on Main Street were relics from the days when Winkler was a lumber town. The store was an ugly cement-colored structure with a flight of wide steps. Will had remodeled the interior to accommodate mining supplies, the mine office and his family. He had also built a separate side entrance to the rooms where he continued to doctor the hill people and the mine families. The other old building was the white frame Methodist Church beside the store. On Sundays about half the Winkler population walked to the Catholic service across the river in Barbara Town.

I left the buggy beside the store steps and carried Freddy inside, where I found women crowding the check-out counter, all talking at once and waving scrip in their hands. Opposite them, Alma stood in a determined stance with her hands spread wide on the counter. Everyone said Alma was a superior clerk, but because of her age, it seemed unfair that these older women were giving her such trouble. I carried Freddy around the store, looking for the manager, Mr. Wise. When I could not find him, I returned to stand beside Alma. Whatever the complaint, it could not be her fault.

My presence did nothing to quiet the women. Alma spoke close to my ear. "Their men work at the Barbara Mine. They want to pay with Barbara Mine scrip, but Mr. Wise told me not to take it anymore because the Barbara won't pay us for it. Mr. Wise has gone to fetch the mail, and Wanda is on a house call with Doc Will. Should I get Mr. Townsend?"

I didn't think we needed a man to help when this was a situation I knew about. The Barbara Town women should be satisfied with a truthful explanation. Paying in scrip was a common practice in the mines, but most operators wanted their scrip spent at their own company stores. I understood why miners and their wives resented the practice. When the Barbara Mine started up, the operator had allowed its employees to redeem their scrip at the Winkler store. But now the Barbara had its own company store.

My attempt to persuade them was lost in the hubbub, and Alma's voice began to quiver. The women reminded me of orphanage children ganging up on a newcomer, a situation made worse when the new child looked different. Alma looked markedly different from the women on the other side of the counter. She was young and pretty with shining black hair, wearing a bright yellow dress, a hand-me-down from Glory. Even my faded garment was a contrast to their limp dark skirts and stained blouses. Most of the women had babies in their arms and young children crowding close.

I leaned across the counter to one who looked no older than Alma. She held a child about the age of Freddy. "Ma'am," I said, "your husband's employer will no longer redeem scrip you spend here. So this store can sell to you for cash only. It's not our fault, but we're sorry."

She looked surprised to be singled out, then spoke in the ear of the one beside her. The clamor died down only for a moment. Exasperated, I struck the counter with my fist. Alma jumped back, and the women quieted. My fist stung. Freddy started to cry, then the child in the arms of the woman across from me wailed too. I passed Freddy to Alma and asked her to take him to his father.

As Alma moved away, one of the women said, "I seen you in church with one of the owners. I guess you figure this is your store? You take whatever you want?"

"I'm May Rose Townsend, and I pay for what I buy. And you are...?"

"You don't care who we are."

Those at the counter now stepped back, making way for an older woman who edged her way to the front. "Ma'am, prices are better here," she said. "Over there, our scrip don't stretch."

Their grumbling died down, and now their faces made me sad.

"*You people*," the first one said. "You people are *evil*. You don't know what it is to live like us."

Her words were like a slap in the face. I knew well what it was to live in hardship, as did Wanda and Alma, Luzanna and Will. Even Barlow had lived rough after the failure of his grocery enterprise. But our histories would not change their opinion. It did not matter that we knew about hard times—we were doing better now. Like other owners, we not only made money from the coal their men dug, but we had rent from the houses they lived in and profits from everything they bought in our store. Most of that income was applied to the mine's indebtedness, but the workers didn't know details like that.

As they backed and turned toward the door, I reached into the candy jar and held out a fistful of licorice sticks. The children understood and stepped forward with outstretched hands. I thought the mothers might object, but they wisely did not, for the candy would make the children less restless on their trek back to Barbara Town. Again I said, "I'm sorry." I knew they resented the candy.

Alma returned with Barlow and Freddy as the women left the store. He held Freddy while she filled my order of cornmeal, canned milk and coffee.

"Alma, if anything like that happens again, call me at once," he said.

"She conducted herself admirably," I said. "I needn't have interfered—I think they would soon have gone. I tried to sweeten their day with candy for the children, about twelve sticks. I'll tell Alma to add it to our bill."

"Wanda hands out candy on occasion," he said. "Let the store pay." While Alma was turned away, he took a sideways step and pressed his arm around my waist, a quick, encouraging grip. He withdrew his arm and we straightened before she turned back.

He carried Freddy when I took my purchases outside to the buggy. On the bottom step, Barlow stopped and gave me a puzzled look. "Where did you leave it?"

The buggy was nowhere to be seen. The street in front of the store was empty of vehicles and pedestrians, and the group of women and children from Barbara Town was only distantly visible, approaching the bridge to Barbara Town. I'd thought their anger might have provoked them to theft, but we saw no buggy with them.

In a few minutes we knew it wasn't stolen at all. We found it in the weedy space behind the store, upside-down with its bedding trampled and dirty, the spokes of its wheels broken and its wicker sides kicked in. The vandalism seemed an expression of hatred, perhaps directed at the Barbara Mine owners but inflicted on my family. It was even more frightening because its target was the carriage that had held my child.

"Oh, Barlow, who would do this?"

"Let's go. I'll carry Freddy and bring the buggy home later."

"It was so beautiful."

"Too beautiful, I think."

The pity I had felt for the Barbara Town women became a small but jagged rock of hatred, even though they might not have been the ones who'd kicked in the buggy's sides. It only took one, maybe the one who had called us evil. Wounded minds did not easily change, including mine.

"I'm sorry you and Alma had to be the focus of their resentment," Barlow said. "The other operators are angry with us too. They want us to raise our store prices."

"I wish the women had just taken the buggy. Any of them could use it."

"It would be discovered," he said.

"And this?"

"I doubt anyone will tell. But if we discover the vandals, what do you want to do?"

"Nothing." The women seemed punished enough.

Like other mining towns that were private property, ours provided its own law enforcement. The Winkler Mine employed four armed guards who worked in shifts through night and day. Barlow said their orders were mainly to prevent theft of equipment, arrest men for brawling and drunkenness, and to shovel horse droppings from the streets. But we'd heard stories of guards in other towns, brutal men with orders to keep miners from congregating, to break up demonstrations of sympathy for the union, and to keep out union organizers.

I took Barlow's arm as we walked uphill together. "Do you know a miner named Karakas?"

"There's a Karakas on our payroll. Fairly new."

I told him about the woman walking her children to the roadhouse. "If I'd given her the buggy, it would still be perfect."

"If you'd like, we'll fix it up and give it to her."

I liked to think he would have done that even if we hadn't been able to afford another.

⊙⫯⫯⊙

LATER THAT DAY, WANDA'S UNCLE RUSSELL AND WILL'S brother Charlie brought the damaged buggy to our back porch.

Evie said the Winkler children made fun of Russell and Charlie—Russell because of his restless eyes and Charlie because he never looked at anyone. They seldom spoke and wore clothes that smelled of the stockyard where they managed the cattle and pigs shipped in by train. I owed Russell a debt of gratitude too great to repay. The older brother of my first husband, Russell had not only made the long train trip to Fargo with Wanda and me, he had twice rescued Charlie, first when the little boy ran away from home, and years later, when Russell found him in jail, beaten and senseless. Then he and Charlie had ridden their horses all the way back to us in Winkler. Not long after Barlow and I moved into our two rooms, Charlie decided he could sleep in a house again, and he and Russell moved from the horse shed to the house where Wanda and I had lived together. Back then, the town was not so crowded, and we'd spent many summer evenings outside at Charlie's campfires. Since Freddy's birth, I'd seen less of them.

Charlie looked fit and handsome, and at times he even looked at me directly, making me think his confusion might be fading. Russell looked old and wild as ever with his long kinky beard and hair, which I suspected was washed only by rain.

"Come for supper," I said. "We'll eat outside."

Russell grunted. Charlie said nothing, but I knew they had accepted. Wanda had said Charlie sometimes came into the store, but was still uneasy under anyone else's roof. We were grateful for the smallest sign of progress.

Barlow came home that evening with the information that a miner named Karakas lived at number 14 Second Street.

I showed him the buggy. "Charlie pounded out the sides, but I'm not sure about giving it away. Mrs. Karakas might think I was giving it to her because it's no longer good enough for me."

"But which is worse," Barlow asked, "to let her remain in need or let her think less of you for giving her a damaged buggy?"

I'd thought of an alternative, a child's wagon displayed on a high store shelf. I did not often reveal my wishes, because Barlow always tried to fulfill them. This time I said what I thought we should do.

That evening with friends around me, Freddy asleep, and my conscience eased, I forgot the harsh words of the woman from the Barbara Mine.

❧

THE NEXT MORNING ONE OF THE NEW STORE CLERKS DELIVERED a child's wagon and Wanda's baby pen, and I learned that Wanda's idea of half a day included most of the morning and afternoon. She brought Otis to the house in his stroller, a vehicle smaller than our buggy and more suitable for an older child.

Wanda recognized Mrs. Karakas from my description, but said she had no time to deliver the wagon to 14 Second Street. My eagerness to help Mrs. Karakas temporarily stopped me from worrying about my new responsibility and what I'd do if I was diapering Freddy at a moment when Otis needed me to save him from danger. My son had taken to squirming away every time I tried to change him, and I could not leave him on the bed alone.

Otis did not like being confined in the pen for more than a few minutes, but Freddy seemed satisfied to sit there and watch the older boy, so all I had to do was keep Otis satisfied.

Luzanna came early in the afternoon with coffee cake and a winter cap she had knitted for Freddy. "I don't know how you find time to do everything," I said.

"I get it done by blessing every job I get and praying there will be more to come." She lifted Otis to a chair at the table and gave him a slice of cake, then set Freddy on her lap and fed crumbles between his lips. "I have an hour to rest. I'll play with these boys if you want to take the wagon to that woman."

When you know and love people, you stop noticing if they're handsome or ugly, or if there's anything odd about them, like a harelip or a withered arm. Luzanna was living evidence for the belief that a woman lost a tooth with every pregnancy. Too many babies had caused her teeth to rot, and no matter how much she ate, she added no softness to her face or form. But her voice was always warm, and the sight of her always made me happy.

I pulled the wagon toward Second Street, hoping for the best. I was certain Mrs. Karakas would take the wagon, and if she resented me because I had seen her need, I would not let myself care. This was for the children.

"I'm looking for Mrs. Karakas," I said, when I reached the house numbered 14. A woman sat on the step, watching four small children play in the leaves, two with fat bottoms that indicated diapers.

"I'm her." She rose and brushed leaf litter from her skirt. "What are you wanting me for?" She was golden haired and looked healthier than the woman I'd met yesterday.

"My name is May Rose. I met another Mrs. Karakas yesterday, on her way to work."

"That would be Etta. She's the widow of my husband's brother. He was killed at the Big Bend. Her and her kids been staying with us. I'm Marie."

Now I understood why Etta walked her children a mile to work and back each day. It wasn't against policy to have more than one family in the company houses, and many miners came with elderly mothers, aunts, and disabled relatives, but I agreed with Will and Glory: so many children should not be crowded together. Burdened as I felt with the care of one child, I could not imagine what it was like for seven small children and three adults in a house of four rooms.

"Is Etta here now?"

The young woman shook her head. "She didn't come back yesterday."

"Didn't come back? And you didn't look for her?"

Marie stooped and pulled leaves from the mouth of one of the smaller children. "I thought she was working late, and I had these four to feed and put to bed. She's a sensible girl. I was sure she was somewhere. She takes good care of her kids."

"I'm sure she does."

"I can't do everything I'd like, you know? I worried some when it got to be dark, but she has a friend at the Big Bend mining camp. She goes there sometimes."

"That far? Walking the children?" The Big Bend Mine was at least three miles west.

"Sometimes she carries two, and they sit and rest a lot. They might of got a ride with somebody."

Mrs. Karakas's two older children had been inching across the lawn. In a sudden, brave advance, they plopped down on the wagon.

"You kids," she said, "get back up here and leave the lady alone."

"It's all right. I brought the wagon for your sister-in-law so her children would not have to walk such distances. Is there anyone who could search to make sure she's all right?"

"My husband will likely do something when he gets home from his shift. That wagon looks new. Are you really gonna leave it here?"

"Yes, I don't need it."

The woman got up and pulled the wagon close to her doorstep. "It's real kind of you, the best thing anybody has done since we got here. Does your husband work for the Winkler Mine?"

"He does."

"The Winkler ain't a bad one, my husband says. He worked at

Big Bend too. We come here a month ago. He says the Big Bend ain't safe."

"I'm sorry about Etta's husband," I said.

"She's got nothing. We're helping all we can, but you know a miner's pay is hardly enough to feed one family, never mind two."

"She gets no compensation from the fund?"

"Ha, that thing. Etta applied near a year ago but she ain't never got it. First they said they didn't get the paperwork, so she did it over again and after a few months they sent it back saying one sheet was missing, which we know darn well was not missing when she sent it in, then they said the company disputed the claim, said the accident was her husband's own fault. Which it wasn't but shouldn't matter anyhow. My husband says it's politics. He says the coal men has a chokehold on ever last thing in the whole state of West Virginia and maybe Washington too. Her claim will be hid in some dusty stack in Charleston and never picked up again."

"She should have a lawyer," I said.

"Well, o'course she should have a lawyer, how else can a poor man or woman get their due? If it was a union mine, there'd be a lawyer could help her. None of us can afford one on our own. My husband said there was union talk at the roadhouse just before we got into the war, and ever last man that spoke up for it was fired and blacklisted."

I'd heard about the blacklist. The Winkler Mine had ignored it because Randolph said the miners in question were among his best workers.

Marie stopped to break up a tussle among her children for the wagon handle, and I left, promising to ask at the store if anyone had seen Etta Karakas. At the orphanage, I'd known too many cases of women and children attacked and abandoned, and one instance of a widow who had drowned herself and her child.

Nearing the store, I saw my husband pause on the steps and

wave. At that moment I believed I could bear up under any kind of news and live anywhere as long as we were together.

He held out his hand and drew me to his side. "What's wrong? Is Freddy all right?"

I told him about Etta Karakas not coming home.

"Randolph offered his automobile so I could drive to the operators' meeting," he said. "I have time to inquire at the roadhouse. Do you have time to ride along?"

"I do." He always seemed to make my needs his priority. I didn't want to know how I compared with his first wife, but living with Barlow magnified the weaknesses of my first husband. Jamie Long had never given a thought to what I needed.

Randolph's automobile had a wide front seat, but as soon as we turned onto the road north, I scooted from the passenger side to the middle and sat close.

All the way to the roadhouse I worried we would find the bodies of Mrs. Karakas and her children in the river. A slow train of coal cars clicked along beside us, blocking our view of the water. At the roadhouse, I waited in Randolph's automobile while Barlow went inside to inquire.

He came out shaking his head. "They fired her yesterday. The bartender didn't like her bringing her kids, and yesterday one of them threw up on the floor."

When I met Etta she hadn't seemed desperate, but with no job, she must be close to getting that way. I could not imagine she'd try to take a sick child all the way to Big Bend.

The train had cleared the tracks, and Barlow drove back slowly so we could watch the roadside and riverbank. We saw her at the same time, lying on a sandy spur of the river, curved around her youngest. The other two children squatted near the water. I choked with relief. Barlow stopped the automobile and we hurried over the tracks and down to the water's edge.

One of the children stood with a warning shout. "Ma!"

We stopped short, noticing a bad odor. Mrs. Karakas sat up

and pulled the baby into her lap. "We been sick," she said. Damp hair hung over her face, and her dress was darkened with bits of something, like one of them had thrown up on her. "I think we're gonna be all right now."

"Can you stand? We have an automobile. We'll take you home," Barlow said.

She pushed back the hair that drooped over her face. "Thank you, but I'm afraid they've dirtied their britches, and I don't want us to mess your clean seats. We'll rest here in the sun and wash off in the river when we feel a little better. It's nice here, and home ain't far off."

"I'll tell your family." Conscious of the plush seats in an automobile that did not belong to us, I did not attempt to persuade her to come. "Are your children hungry?" If Luzanna could stay with Otis and Freddy, I might return with the child's wagon and something to eat.

"Oh, no. I doubt our stomachs is ready for food."

"I'll send the doctor," Barlow said.

"Please don't bother the doctor. It's only something going around."

I hadn't heard of anything going around, but according to Wanda, miners and their families always knew more about everyone. "Someone will come for you soon," I said.

Barlow opened the automobile door and took my hand to help me step to the running board. Looking back, I saw Mrs. Karakas at the river's edge, wetting the hem of her skirt and wiping a child's face. One of the children waved goodbye as we drove away. I waved and watched until they were gone from sight.

"I'll ask Russell to hitch up his wagon and bring them home," Barlow said.

"Oh, that's a good idea, thank you. I'd gladly bring her the child's wagon, for as Etta said, town isn't far from here, but I don't like to impose on Luzanna to stay too long with Freddy and Otis."

"It's best you don't get too involved. You can't save every mother and child."

Wanda had said the same thing for years. "I can't help trying. When I see Etta Karakas struggling to keep her children alive— as Luzanna was doing when we met—I think of myself, how desperate I'd have been if Jamie had left me with a child or two."

"We'll do what we can for this one," he said.

"I promise I won't start inviting widows and orphans to live with us. But there must be other ways to help. Mrs. Karakas applied for compensation a year ago. Her sister-in-law thinks she'll never get it."

"She's probably right."

"You think so? She'll get nothing?"

"Our workers' compensation system is a fraud. The governor appointed a coal operator as its commissioner, which unfortunately explains everything. Companies are supposed to contribute to the fund according to the number of workers they employ, but I've heard operators brag they've never paid and never will. There's never been enough money in the fund for all who should have it."

"But the Winkler Mine pays?"

He nodded. "Most mines in our association are owned by far-away investors who know only the amounts of their checks and believe what the operators tell them. To be fair, I doubt investors know anything of miners' lives. How would they? I haven't met any owners who live in their mining towns, as we do."

We were riding along at a nice speed that cooled us with the breeze and made me hold onto my hat. I should have enjoyed this break in my day and been glad that Etta and her children were safe, but I couldn't put aside the injustice of her situation.

"Does no one see that what is good for one side might possibly be good for the other?"

"We do," Barlow said. "Randolph believes when the men are

proud of their work and understand we're all in this business together, they're better at it."

"I'm glad you're a fair employer."

"I have no choice. I'm afraid of my wife."

He was driving with only one hand on the wheel and the other arm over my shoulder. I brought his free hand to my lips. He did not stop watching the road, but I saw his grin.

He slowed the automobile as we came into town. "Mrs. Karakas might have better luck if she applied for a Mother's Pension. It's a state program that started a couple of years ago. Tell her to come to my office and I'll help her with the paperwork. With three children, she should be eligible for the full amount. I think that's 25 dollars a month."

The amount was probably a quarter of what her husband had earned, but it might keep them from starving.

I was eager to relieve Luzanna and check on Freddy, who'd been exposed yesterday to children who'd since fallen sick. But for once my uneasiness about my child was replaced by concern for someone else. "I hate to think of Etta being badly used. And the children."

"And we hate paying into the compensation fund when others don't. We've talked about setting up something for our mine only."

"Would you do that instead of contributing to the state compensation fund?"

"Impossible," he said. "Should an accident injure or kill several men, compensating them would bankrupt us. That's why we need to be in an insurance group with many people, and why the other operators should be made to cooperate. At present there's no enforcement."

"So if you had a local fund it would be extra, a way to help a little."

"Whatever we could afford," he said.

"Maybe the miners could elect a committee to distribute assistance."

Barlow frowned and chuckled at the same time. "The association operators would have a fit. They're against any freely-elected committee as well as any benefits they haven't agreed to."

"What could they do about it?"

He shook his head. "Something dirty."

"Because you let the miners choose a committee?"

"The operators would liken it to the union welfare fund. They'd see the committee as a tool for promoting the union."

"If I risked my life for no more than five dollars a day and my employer had no scruples, I'd want somebody to make him do what's right," I said. "A union, if that was the only way."

"The union will come. When the war ends, the men will ask for the union and a decent wage, and when they don't get either, they'll go out on strike. I hope the process will be peaceful, but there's a good chance it won't."

"Would you be able to pay 60 cents a ton?"

Barlow turned uphill toward our house, driving slower on the dirt surface. "May Rose, I don't like to worry you with these things."

"And I don't want to live in ignorance. Will you be able to pay the union wage?"

He shook his head. "The sad thing is, we could pay more than 25 cents now and we should be doing it, but there's no way we can afford 60 a ton unless we can sell coal at a higher rate. We don't know what the market will be after the war, nor the costs of freight. And we can't assume our miners won't walk out."

He stopped the automobile in front of our house and we sat there a moment, looking at its tall brick front and the boards nailed over the upper story window openings.

"Don't let the other operators stop you from helping people," I said. "I'll be your welfare fund committee, and get Luzanna to help. If we take care of people, when the time comes, your miners might not want to strike. They might turn the union men away."

"I'll talk with Randolph and Will," he said, "because giving aid is a good thing to do. But no matter how good we try to be, there will always be workers who are as greedy and stubborn as the owners, and they'll always press for more. Not all of our miners will want to strike, but they'll have no choice. Even if they're better off here, they'll be sympathetic to bad situations of men in the other mines. They'll stick together."

"The few should not control lives of the many," I said. But I felt certain it had always been so.

CHAPTER 7

A week later, our town was the scene of a third general registration for the draft. While the earlier sign-ups were for men between the ages of 21 and 31, the third required the registration of men as young as 18 and as old as 45, a range that included Will, Charlie, and Randolph. Some might have thought it patriotic, but I hated the sight of almost all the men of Winkler lined up on the street, waiting to identify themselves as warriors for a war an ocean away. According to the newspaper, the same thing was going on all over the country. I feared the need for so many men meant our soldiers were being killed and maimed in great numbers.

Barlow maintained that registration in a mining town was a useless exercise, because the local draft board knew better than to pick off men from the coal association. I worried, though, because Will was not exactly vital to the mine operation—he was the mine doctor, and we knew the war needed doctors. Someone on the draft board might decide to do the right thing, which would be very wrong for us.

Will had told Barlow that if he was selected, he would not try to avoid serving, but that was before he'd known about Grady

Malone. I had another selfish reason to pray the draft board did not select Will, for who could predict what a lonely wife might do in her husband's absence? My greatest worry was for Charlie, who had no claim to exempt status unless Will could convince the draft board his brother had suffered memory loss and was subject to fits of violence. Poor Charlie. He hadn't always been so.

৩৯৩

MY NEWEST MOTIVE FOR GETTING BACK TO CHURCH WAS AN unspoken wish to see Grady Malone, the man who threatened Wanda's family, or at least her reputation. Such curiosity went against my better judgment, for seeing him would not help Wanda and Will.

At the church steps, Barlow carried Freddy through the men's door on the left, while I passed through the door on the right and joined them inside. The new preacher had tried to get the congregation to follow the old tradition of separate seating for men and women, but had given up because the families were large and parents needed to sit together to manage the children.

Barlow removed his hat and motioned toward an empty space in a pew not far from the back, where we could easily leave if Freddy reverted to his old behavior. The fact that I worried about him disrupting the service made me wonder what was wrong with me, for there were many whimpering infants and restless children kicking and wiggling in the pews. I was sure the service had always been like that, but it hadn't seemed a disturbance until I had my own small contributor.

Fortunately, being among many people held Freddy's attention. As soon as we were settled, I looked to see if Wanda had arrived. The church floor sloped down from the doors behind us to a raised platform in front, which was surrounded by a low rail. If not for the slope, I wouldn't have seen much, for the congregation was a sea of women's wide-brimmed hats, interspersed with bare heads of men and children.

One head in the crowd was different, a hatless crown of hair so pale it was nearly white, loosely curled and flowing over the shoulders of a young woman who was twisting in her seat, smiling and scanning the faces of everyone present like she was looking for someone or wanted someone to smile back. She smiled at me too, or so I thought. The look I returned was probably startled, because she braced her hand on the shoulder of a man with a bald head and fringe of reddish hair, our friend Simpson. She had to be his daughter, Blanche. They sat halfway to the front, Simpson on the center aisle. She was well worth the notice, pale with startling blue eyes and an expression that said she was not only delighted to see everyone, but loved each one so much she could barely keep to her seat.

She didn't keep her seat when Wanda and her family arrived. Will nodded to us as he passed our row and followed Wanda, Otis, and Evie down the aisle toward an empty row near the front. Before they reached their seats, Blanche squeezed past her father, hurried after them and captured Wanda in a hug.

Around us, the hum of talk hushed. We were too far away to hear their conversation, but we saw Wanda push down on Blanche's arms, releasing herself. Children in the pews stopped knocking about and gave their eager attention to what might be the start of a fight. At the same time three men stepped to the platform. One went to the piano and the others approached the high-backed chairs at either side of the platform.

Simpson left his pew and hurried to his daughter in the aisle. Because he blocked my view, I couldn't tell if he was greeting Wanda and Will or trying to avoid a disturbance. When Wanda and her family moved on down the aisle, he took Blanche's arm and turned her back to her seat. Someday his wife might need to share details of Wanda's kidnapping to explain why Wanda had not given his daughter a kinder greeting.

I didn't identify the teacher until he rose to lead the congregation in the first hymn. Grady Malone looked like an ordinary working man, thin under a shapeless black suit and topped by shaggy brown hair, but he sang like an angel, smooth, high and sweet.

I held the hymnbook and Barlow jiggled Freddy in his arms, neither of us attempting to sing. Though the congregation sang loudly and with vigor, I easily detected Wanda's voice, for it was as strong and flowing as Grady's. The effect was like a duet, with the voices of the congregation no more than background. Grady stood beside the piano with his shoulders straight and his chin lifted, staring toward Wanda's side of the church. I was relieved not to see her face, afraid it might be an embarrassing reflection of the teacher's. I needed to know very soon that she and her husband were in harmony too.

<hr/>

AFTER CHURCH, SIMPSON APPROACHED US OUTSIDE AND introduced his daughter. Ruby, oldest of his grandchildren, stood close to his side, holding his hand. I hadn't noticed Ruby in the pew, and was surprised because I thought she was with Piney at Lucie's, several hours away.

"I went and got Ruby," Simpson said. "I promised Piney I'd do it if they wasn't back by the startup of school. She didn't want Ruby to miss out."

"You gotta pretty baby," Blanche said, pinching the toe of one of Freddy's blue booties. "Pretty as his ma."

"Thank you," I said. Ruby left her grandfather and slid her hand into mine. Her eyes always had a pinched, worried look. Before I married Barlow she'd been the youngest in my class of six pupils, and she'd learned her letters while sitting on my lap.

Wanda and Will passed through the crowd with no more than a nod in our direction.

"I been living in big places," Blanche said, staring after Wanda and Will. "I might go back." She turned away and moved through the crowd. In a moment we saw she'd joined a circle of women around Grady Malone.

Simpson frowned after her, then turned back to us and took Ruby's other hand. "May Rose, I need a favor. Two favors. Could Ruby come to your house after school, just until I finish work for the day? I can't count on Blanche to be at home."

"She'll be very welcome." Ruby was never difficult. She was old enough to fetch and carry, and she loved to help.

"There's another thing," he said. "Could you take Blanche to your get-together next Saturday? She hasn't got a single friend, and she's restless. Walks out at all times of the day and night. I'm afraid she's gonna bolt."

Simpson knew his daughter was difficult, but he could have no idea how Blanche's presence would change our gathering. Wanda, especially, would hate it and might stay away, but for his sake I had to try. "I'll call for her next Saturday. We'll see how she gets along."

Simpson leaned down and pressed both of his large hands around mine. He kept his head down for a moment, and when he raised it, his eyes were shiny with tears.

BOTH VIRGIE AND GLORY HAD GOOD BUSINESS SENSE, BARLOW said, so Sunday evening we invited them to our house for a conversation about a welfare fund for Winkler Mine employees. Barlow asked his partners to attend as well, but only Randolph came. Randolph Bell was always the most pleasing and entertaining guest, just as he was said to be the most serious and industrious at work. That evening he looked smarter and better groomed than usual, and I suspected he had worked a stiff brush into the creases of his hands, which on most days were stained by coal dust. Unlike Barlow and Will, he regularly went down in the mine.

This was to be an informal meeting, and I'd prepared for company by washing my face and removing my apron. Virgie, however, took the opportunity to wear her new beaded jacket. With no one to take care of but themselves, Virgie and Glory had more time to look their best. They could have spent their days in leisure, because Virgie had a small income from her late husband, and Glory had an inheritance from Hester Townsend. Instead, they'd chosen to be dressmakers.

Glory needed no extra effort to make herself attractive, for she had the smooth skin and bright eyes of youth. While Virgie was talkative and animated in the presence of eligible men, Glory remained quiet and composed. Barlow wished she would settle down with someone responsible like Randolph, but if she ever thought about him or any man, she kept those thoughts to herself.

Prior to the start of our discussion, Virgie attempted to stimulate a conversation between Randolph and Glory by telling him of Glory's concern for the health of miners' children. Randolph listened to Virgie while sending appreciative glances to Glory, who looked like she wished the conversation were more about the children and less about herself.

After these moments of sociability, Barlow ushered us to the table under our sugar maple. First, he discussed the problems of the state's compensation fund, then the difficulties that would ensue if the Winkler Mine tried to establish a fund of its own.

"There's an advantage to being part of a big system," he said. "It spreads the risk. To have our own fund, either we buy insurance or become our own insurance company. Both would have greater costs."

"You should get some credit for having a safe operation," Glory said. "You've had only one injury and no deaths in two years. If you establish your own insurance, surely you'd have time to build up a reserve."

Randolph shifted on the bench. "Anything can happen. One man gets careless and we have a disaster."

We sat for a moment with solemn faces.

"Alone, we can't provide full compensation," Barlow said. "So our welfare program should not replace what we pay to the state fund. I'm thinking of something less. Charitable assistance."

"All families need something," Virgie said. "How would you decide who gets what? Whatever you do, plenty will gripe that someone who didn't need it got help and they didn't."

"It won't be easy work, dividing a limited amount of assistance, determining how it might be given, how often, and to whom," Barlow said.

I drew a breath, imagining trouble—disagreements and complaints of favoritism. But I also thought of Etta Karakas. It was worth doing, and better than doing nothing.

Randolph asked, "Should we have some miners' wives on this committee?"

He blushed when Glory directed her response to him. "In the long run, I think it would be good, but we don't know them well enough to determine who would be fair and discreet. I suppose the wives could elect them, maybe from their Ladies' Aid group at the church. We'd also need a representative from the Catholic's Altar Society."

"We should be committed to a plan before we approach anyone," I said.

Randolph nodded his agreement. "Otherwise they'll resent us even more." He was supposedly a much-admired boss. I was surprised to hear he felt resented too.

Our agenda for the next women's gathering at Virgie's was to knit socks for soldiers and talk about ideas for the Winkler Mine's welfare plan. I warned my friends that I would be bringing Blanche Cotton. Wanda said she didn't care, which meant she wouldn't be attending. The others agreed we needed to include Blanche as a way to help Simpson.

My days were now less lonely, for Wanda chatted a few minutes when she brought Otis. Luzanna often stopped mid-morning for coffee, and Evie and Ruby came after school, Evie to take Otis home and Ruby to stay until the end of Simpson's work day. All I needed was more space in the house, but as long as the weather was good, our living area expanded to the back porch and the yard.

Barlow had hired Luzanna to help out when I got nothing done but walk all day with Freddy in my arms. I supposed I could now manage on my own, even with the addition of Otis, but I did not like to take those few dollars from her income. She also came to our house and used our wringer washer to launder sheets and clothing for the town's bachelors. Luzanna found other ways to help us, and usually I felt in her debt.

She had an idea about work for Mrs. Karakas. "I know a house that must be a fright and two men who are well able to pay a woman to clean and such."

"Russell and Charlie," I said. "But they turned you down. I can't see them tolerating a stranger."

"I expect Wanda could get them to do it."

Luzanna was right. Russell was rough and short of speech, but he'd always had a soft spot for Wanda, and Charlie seemed more at ease with her than with anyone else. I thought it was worth a try. I asked her the next morning.

Wanda tolerated no obstacles. "I'll just tell Uncle Russell he has to hire help. It'll be okay as long as him and Charlie ain't in the house when Etta is. What do you think, two days a week? But she better do a good job and not steal nothing. I'll be checking."

The next Saturday afternoon, I escorted Blanche to Virgie's house. She asked what I was carrying. "It's my workbasket," I said. "Today we're knitting socks for soldiers."

"I never took to knitting," she said, "but I knowed some soldiers."

The others greeted her kindly, and for a while she dominated the talk by asking each if they had children and husbands and telling us how this woman named Piney had married her father, as though we didn't know. "My kids' pa is dead, but they have a good grandpap," she said.

We agreed.

"And a good granny," Luzanna said.

"I 'spose." Blanche sat on one of Virgie's needlepoint-padded chairs with her hands in her lap and her ankles crossed and told us the names of her children—Ruby, Robert, Ralphie—while we nodded as though we hadn't known them all these years. At last Virgie took charge of the discussion.

"Randolph has asked us to keep this topic among ourselves, because we don't know for sure what we'll be doing, and we don't want wrong information getting out."

"All right." Blanche made a sign of locking her lips. "What don't we want to get out?"

"Ideas," I said, suddenly wary. "Ways we can help people."

"That's so nice. I love helping people. Who are you going to help?"

Virgie narrowed her eyes. "Let's not name names. We might all think on it this week and come up with rules."

My friends and I nodded in agreement. Blanche should not be included in confidential discussions.

She wiggled on the chair like she could not wait to begin. "Rules?"

"Anything you can think of," Glory said. "Perhaps we should talk today about helping the war effort. Women of the Ladies' Aid have been collecting old clothes for Belgian refugees. Coats and the like."

We'd discussed the clothing drive earlier and had already left our donations at the church. Virgie was stalling our welfare discussion.

Blanche laughed. "Folks in this town don't have anything but old clothes, and their really old stuff is rags. Except Miss Virgie and Miss Glory. You wear beautiful things. If any of your things is old, I'll take 'em."

We could not help smiling.

Virgie sighed. "Then there's peach pits and walnut shells. The season for peaches is nearly past, of course, but it soon will be time to gather walnuts, and I'm told school children will be going door to door to collect the shells. Remember to save yours."

Blanche said, "Huh?"

"Fruit pits and walnut shells are used in gas masks," Glory said. "In the war, you know, to protect our soldiers."

"Oh. Pa said all them men that lined up on the street the other day is gonna be soldiers."

"I don't think that's what he meant," Glory said. "The men had to register in the event that any future call-up is necessary. It's doubtful even one of them will have to serve. Randolph says he expects the war to be over before winter."

Virgie raised her eyebrows. "Randolph?"

"We spoke briefly after church," Glory said.

While I wondered about Randolph and Glory, she showed Blanche a newspaper with a photo of a gas mask and explained how the pits and shells were ground and turned into charcoal to filter dangerous fumes. In spite of her assurance that no one from Winkler would be drafted, I was sure she must also be worrying about her brothers. And maybe Randolph, too.

Though we didn't approve Blanche's history of neglecting her children, her delight in being with us made her hard to dislike. "I don't want to leave her out," Virgie said, when she, Glory, and Luzanna came to our house later that evening.

We agreed to continue to include Blanche in our sewing circle, but to have a separate meeting for the welfare committee.

We sat at the table in the yard while Glory listed our ideas to discover people's needs, how we might choose among many who needed help, and whether the assistance would be in cash or store credit. There were always families with fathers unable to work and many with large debts at the store. Luzanna said there was probably more than one woman in town who might like cash to get away from a husband who beat her. And if we helped a family with a father who drank most of his wages, would that not free him to drink even more?

"It's all right," Glory said. "We shouldn't expect this to be easy."

OUR NEXT GATHERING AT VIRGIE'S WAS CANCELLED IN FAVOR OF September's Trading Days. With winter approaching, Luzanna expected to sell many pairs of gloves. Virgie and Glory also had a table on the street where they offered their own gently-worn creations at prices favorable to wives of farmers, who unlike the miners, had a bit of money to spend.

Because Saturday was mild, Barlow and I took Freddy downtown in the afternoon, passing tables of food and sellers of liquor-laced medicinal remedies, traders in hides and ginseng, a shoe cobbler, harness maker, knife sharpener, and more. The variety of products and faces was a welcome change from the dullness of ordinary days, and sellers talked up their products in a friendly way.

But Trading Days had changed in ways that worried Will, who'd started the monthly market when he was the town's only resident. It was still the favorite event for socializing, but the increased numbers flocking to town included families from other coal towns and quite a few rowdy young men. Will didn't know how to put an end to the market or how to reform it to its safer and more peaceful past. In the days when the town had the entire valley for wagons and overnight campfires, he'd lit the street with torches and allowed music until dawn. This time he'd posted signs everywhere announcing the market would end when the mine whistle blew, and visitors should be on their way home by dusk. To help with enforcement, he'd given six miners extra work as guards. Barlow observed that young men from other communities created the most trouble, for when they were away from home even good boys tended to forget their upbringing.

The new guards were prominent on the street, all with shiny badges pinned to their shirts, watching the crowd and stopping to talk with groups of young men.

We paused to buy at a table of enticing pastries sold by a dark-skinned woman who stood behind her table with three children. A girl of eight or nine told us how much to pay and counted our money while her mother wrapped two sweet rolls in a sheet of newspaper. The mother looked happy, her children seemed well-behaved, and the exchange left me with the impression that someday I would have friends among the miners' wives.

I intended to stop and see the garments Virgie and Glory were displaying for sale, but could not get near. In addition to being brightly dressed, both wore graceful straw hats that complimented their rounded cheeks and rosy lips. Women stood two and three deep at the front and sides of their table and a group of young men stood a short distance behind, uttering low whistles each time Glory or Virgie held up a jacket or dress for examination.

"Barlow," I said. Charlie was among the men watching the women at the table. In the two years since their reunion, Charlie had established no familiarity with Glory or Will, yet the look on his face said he was bothered by the interest of those young men.

If any should make an improper advance, I feared what he might do.

Barlow did not need an explanation. "Stay here a moment." He left me with Freddy, disappeared in the crowd, and returned a few minutes later with a guard. When the guard moved toward the young men, they dispersed, laughing and shoving each other. Barlow spoke to Charlie, and I sighed in relief.

"I thanked him for watching out for Glory," Barlow said when he returned. "And asked him to call a guard if he thought she or Virgie were being bothered by anyone."

"I hope he'll do that." Glory was probably in danger of no more than rude talk, but if the men had approached their table, Charlie might have seen them as a threat. The real danger was in what he might have done. Russell usually stayed near to moderate Charlie's behavior, but Russell was nowhere to be seen. He liked crowds even less than Charlie did.

I hung onto Barlow's arm as he navigated the stroller past tight and noisy knots of men and boys. "Games of chance," he said, speaking close to my ear. I could not see the game tables, but heard the intermittent roars of suffering and delight. He lifted Freddy from the stroller, an unsafe conveyance because of children running through the crowd and so many men unsteady on their feet.

On a low stage of rough lumber, a man with a guitar appeared to accompany the singing of a woman and two girls. Because of the crowd noise, their music was indistinct.

I touched Barlow's sleeve and pointed to Wanda, who stood with Will, Evie and Otis on the sidewalk in front of the church. Will had his hand behind his ear and was leaning toward a man stepping down from the stage. I didn't identify the man until he turned with a sideways gesture toward the performers. He was the song leader I'd seen in church: Grady Malone. I stopped, but Barlow, pushing the stroller and holding Freddy, walked on without noticing. Accompanied by a feeble slap of applause, the performers left the stage. Grady held his hand out to Wanda. She shook her head.

I caught up to Barlow as Grady stepped to the street and faced Will. "Let her sing!" Startled by Grady's booming voice, people nearby stopped talking. The crowd flowing around us turned to look.

"Let her? She's free to do so," Will said.

"She's not free a'tall. She sees you don't want her to do it. You're stifling her talent, keeping her tied to the house, your nice little housewife."

Embarrassed as I was to witness such a confrontation, I could not help smiling at Grady's notion that anyone could stifle Wanda.

He reached for her hand but Wanda put her arms behind her back and lifted her chin. "Mr. Malone, when I say 'no' you can be sure that's my meaning, and mine alone."

Those watching Grady and Wanda now turned as a commotion stirred in the crowd, men and women stepping back and bumping into each other. "I think there's a fight somewhere," Barlow said. "And guards are breaking up the games." To get out of the way, we backed against the stage with Will and Wanda.

She laughed close to my ear. "Wild horses couldn't make me sing for this crowd."

CHAPTER 8

Our welfare discussions continued through the next week without Wanda, who was working in the store and sometimes accompanying Will on house calls. "He likes me to go if the patient is a woman," she said, "especially if there's a baby on the way. He says I'll make a good midwife."

Her piano had arrived and she'd found a woman from Barbara Town who would come to the store and teach both her and Evie to play. When I asked if she was still practicing with Grady, her reply wasn't really what I wanted to hear. "Oh, now and then," she said. "Don't worry about him." I hoped her ambitions were satisfied.

Our circle had drawn up a list of guidelines for charitable assistance, and Barlow and his partners had approved a budget. Glory thought we might wait until we added miners' wives to the committee before coming up with a way to choose recipients. For some reason my friends thought I was the best one to approach the Ladies' Aid.

"Oh, please, I'd be tongue-tied. Glory would explain our cause so much better."

"Glory's an awful good talker," Virgie said, "but them women won't give credit to the ideas of someone so young. Who's not married. Who's been to college and wears pretty dresses and decides things for herself. Worst of all, who lives in my house."

"There's no disputing Virgie's wisdom," Glory said. "May Rose, we know you'll explain everything in a nice way."

It might have been a good moment to explain how I had failed to explain in a nice way to the Barbara Town women, but that explanation would have awakened my resentment and sparked some of theirs. I put my assignment off for a few days while silently forming a speech to some unknown representative of the Ladies' Aid. At times I imagined her stern and uncooperative, and at other times I allowed her to be gracious and helpful.

Midweek, I left Freddy in Barlow's care after our evening meal and walked to the store to ask Wanda if she could suggest a good candidate. The fall day had been sunny and dry, and the orange and red leaves and a gentle wind made the walk a pleasure. Others were out walking too, and men and women greeted me in a cordial way, making me believe the residents of Winkler did not think we were evil.

Evie sat on the store steps watching Otis, who was pushing his stroller in the street. In her coloring and calm nature, Evie favored her father, the red-haired, freckle-faced boy who'd come to Winkler looking for work when it was a lumber town.

I found Wanda in the store, washing dishes. She had no separate kitchen, just the stove and sink in a front corner of the store, and she still cooked an occasional meal and fed travelers at the table that now served her family.

"Ma! Come and see it!" I followed her to a shining black piano in a rear corner of the store. She fitted a brass key in the lock, lifted the cover over the ivories, stretched her fingers and set them down, striking four tones at once.

"It has a wonderful sound," I said.

"Evie's gonna be better than me. Maybe she'll play for me to sing someday. She doesn't love singing like I do."

Wanda lowered the cover and turned the key. "If I don't keep this thing locked, every kid that comes in here bangs on it. I don't mind them having fun, but they fight over it, and all that commotion bothers other folks."

"You can have musical evenings like Hester did in the boardinghouse."

"Maybe." Wanda slid her arm through mine as we walked to the front of the store. "Having the piano has made me want to live in a house with a parlor like the old boardinghouse, you know? But sometimes I'm sure we'll never live anywhere but here. It's awful convenient to work and all. I doubt we'll build up on the hill like we thought."

I was sorry to hear it, for I'd loved the thought of having her family just one lawn away. While I helped dry and put away the dishes, I told her about the welfare committee's idea to recruit a representative from the Ladies' Aid.

"You know," she said, "A lot of those women are big gossips. Blanche come into the store when a bunch was here. After she left, you should've heard how they went on about her."

"Oh, poor Simpson. What did they say?"

"I never heard them say anything about her running off and leaving the kids for her pa to raise, so maybe they don't know about that. But they said plenty about how she flirts with their men."

"She must be a constant worry to Simpson, so pretty, and so much like a child," I said.

"I can't feel mad at her anymore—I doubt she can help herself. But those women in the Ladies' Aid ain't friendly to me, either. Probably don't think I'm good enough for their handsome doctor. I wouldn't be surprised if some of them started that nonsense about me and Grady."

"So we should not include a miner's wife on our welfare committee?"

"What I'm saying is that telling a thing to one of them might be the same as telling the whole town, especially if it comes from outsiders like us. Makes no difference that we were here first—we don't belong. And here's something else could screw up the works —I'd say about half the women in the Ladies' Aid are from Barbara Town, meaning their husbands work for the Barbara Mine. The welfare is just for Winkler miners, right?"

Only the river separated our two mining towns. Barbara Mine families attended the Winkler church and their children came to the Winkler school. "Everyone has need," I said. "It's too bad everyone can't benefit. Do you suppose the Barbara operators would contribute to the fund?"

"That's a real nice idea but it hasn't got a chance. Will says we need to keep the fund quiet, because the other operators won't like it."

It seemed very hard to do something good.

"I'm thinking a teacher might be the best choice for your committee," Wanda said. "Teachers know the kids and they learn stuff about their families."

I was afraid she was going to name Grady, but she said, "Evie's teacher, Miss Graves, is a good one. She's in that Ladies' Aid but I never hear her talk about anybody."

Wanda assured me she would recruit Miss Graves for the committee and bring her to our next meeting.

On my way from the store I paused on the steps to see what was making everyone stop and look. Children ran from their game of Kick the Can and joined a gathering of adults. All appeared to watch a young soldier walking up the middle of the street, carrying a duffel bag over his shoulder.

Evie rose from the steps. "It's that boy Alma is sweet on," she said. "Patrick O'Neill."

"Alma has a sweetheart?" I shaded my eyes to see the soldier boy who might be one of Luzanna's worries.

Otis trotted off toward the group greeting the soldier, and Evie got up and brought him back. "Alma would like him to be.

He was a year ahead of her in school. She says he favors some other girl. Does this mean the war's over?"

"Maybe. I don't know." It felt good to see the smiles as the soldier shook hands and exchanged greetings. A homecoming was always a fine thing. "This will be a grand day for his family," I said. He looked like a nice boy, but I wondered how much Luzanna had told Alma about appearances.

⚛

THREE DAYS LATER WANDA BROUGHT OTIS TO THE HOUSE WITH shattering news. The O'Neill family's joy at having their soldier boy home had turned to horror.

"Pat O'Neill, that boy who came home on leave? He's dead. And it was bad."

"Dead?" Luzanna sat at the table with me, drinking coffee. Her cup clattered in its saucer. "Was he shot?" It wasn't uncommon to hear of someone shot in the woods, where there were always too many hunters stalking squirrel, deer, or turkey. Brawls at the roadhouse had also been known to end in spilled blood.

While Wanda stared like she'd lost her train of thought, Otis climbed out of his stroller.

"Sit, I'll pour you a coffee," I said.

She blinked and waved away my offer. "Not shot. The boy sickened, just like that. The family says he came home fine, then started a cold. Will says he's never seen the like of it."

In the baby pen, Freddy was on his knees, reaching, bouncing and gripping the bars, trying to pull himself as high as Otis, who was now trying to climb in.

Luzanna lifted Otis and put him in the pen beside Freddy. "Poor Alma. She's gonna take this hard. She's talked a lot about that boy, how smart, how nice. Just yesterday she said he visited the school, so handsome and proud in his uniform."

"He was in awful pain at the end," Wanda said. "Will said the boy's face turned black and he coughed blood all over himself."

Luzanna and I said together, "What was it?"

Wanda opened the door to leave. She took a last look at Otis. "Will can't figure it out."

❦

LUZANNA AND I DECIDED TO VISIT THE BEREAVED FAMILY together. When Evie arrived after school that day, I asked her to stay with Freddy, Otis and Ruby while I delivered a batch of pigs-in-blankets to the O'Neills. I met Luzanna and Alma on the street and followed them to a house that had a stream of visitors going in and out.

Since we were not acquainted, our visit was formal, but the family graciously invited us in and we sat to express our sorrow and listen to the mother talk about her boy. The undertaker still had his body, but it was to be brought to the house the next day for the wake. Luzanna and I sat with Alma between us, holding her hands. She didn't cry, but I felt her trembling.

Barlow came home that evening with a name for the boy's sudden death. "Hemorrhagic pneumonia," he said. "But the diagnosis doesn't explain its rapid course. Pneumonia usually takes people who are old and sick, and it never strikes so fast. Will thinks the boy may have been attacked by something else."

Barlow accompanied Luzanna and Alma to the Catholic funeral, which he said drew mourners from several mine towns. The soldier was oldest of six sons. There must be consolation, I thought, in having many children.

Luzanna frequently reminded me that most of what we worried about never came to pass, but I wondered if it might be better if a mother's hopes were not pinned on an only child. When Freddy was born, the doctor had said it was unlikely I would have another. I still hoped. Another doctor had predicted I'd not have even one.

❦

IN ONE SENSE, I HAD OTHER CHILDREN—WANDA, CHARLIE, and Will, for I'd cared for all of them when they were young. Luzanna said Wanda dumped her troubles on me because she thought of me as her ma. "Once my kids tell me their problems they feel better. Of course then I feel worse," she said. "You'll see: nothing's ever as bad as they let on."

Wanda was currently troubled about Charlie. "It's that Blanche," she said. "She's trying to get her hooks into him."

"Where do you see Blanche and how do you know she favors Charlie?"

"In the store of course. Blanche walks the streets all day. We have to watch her like a hawk so she don't walk out with stuff. Simpson don't trust her to buy anything. He gets the groceries and I'll bet since Piney's been away he's done the cooking. Little Ruby's more responsible than her ma, but she's a bit dim, too, wouldn't you say?"

Ruby might be a slow learner, but already she seemed more reliable than her mother. "Have you seen Blanche with Charlie?"

"No, but Simpson was talking about them. He said her and Charlie met when he came to the mill for cracked corn. Charlie and Russell is fattening a pig."

"Does Charlie like her?"

"Of course he don't, who would? And if he does, I'll tell him not to."

"Wanda, you can't do that."

"I know, but it's gonna be hard. Just think, Ma. Blanche is a wily creature and Charlie ain't got half..." She stopped. "I mean, Charlie don't know a good woman from the other kind."

"We don't know what he knows," I said. But she'd given me a new worry.

Blanche created a small disturbance at my house the next day. Evie had left with Otis and I'd taken Freddy and Ruby outside for some fresh air.

Blanche came into the yard. "Ruby, there you are, you bad girl!" Blanche was teasing, but her daughter looked frightened.

"Come along home now," Blanche said.

Ruby shrank from Blanche's outstretched hand. "I'm supposed to stay here until Pap comes."

"But I'm your ma, and I say 'come.'"

"Ruby," I said, "please take Freddy into the house."

When the door shut behind them, I turned to Blanche.

"She needs to mind me," Blanche said.

"I think she needs to mind Simpson and Piney, because they take care of her now, and they've been doing that for a long time. You left her, remember?"

Blanche's face looked as confused as Ruby's. "I just want her to like me."

"She will. Just do what your pa says."

"He'll be home soon. I don't see why she can't go with me now."

"He's your pa, and he says Ruby should wait for him. You should mind what he says."

"All right. But can I wait too?"

"You may. Sit right there at the table."

Blanche sat, and I brought Ruby and Freddy outside again. For a while, Blanche seemed content to watch them sitting on a blanket, passing Freddy's toys back and forth. Then abruptly she got up and left. I doubted she would ever stay in one place long enough for her daughter to trust her.

I KNEW OUR CHARITABLE ASSISTANCE WOULD LIKELY GIVE US more problems than satisfactions, and though I told myself I was doing this for women like Etta Karakas, I was aware of a selfish motive. Helping even a little would make me feel less guilty about being better off.

The next Saturday our sewing circle dismissed early so we could meet our new member and discuss the welfare fund. I walked with Blanche as far as her father's house, then hurried back to Virgie's. Wanda was already there, introducing Miss Bertha Graves, the teacher.

"Miss Graves is in the Ladies' Aid and she boards with Mr. and Mrs. Greggorio," Wanda said. "Her landlady knows everybody and is Catholic to boot. So we kinda got a member with ties to each camp."

Miss Graves was a plain-looking young woman who looked no older than Alma. "I'm happy to hear about your welfare proposal," she said, "for there's great need. My landlady has two daughters married to miners right here in Winkler. They don't have much themselves, you understand, but Mrs. Greggorio and her daughters do what they can to help any who are less fortunate. When I fretted about a child who came to school in rags, they made over a dress and a coat for her and tied them up in a package with a red ribbon from one of their hats. How the child prized that ribbon! So much around these children is bleak and black."

Wanda was right; already Miss Graves had revealed needs as well as generous aspects of the miners' wives that we hadn't suspected. Her enthusiasm made us more confident about the importance of our project, and I was relieved of the task of approaching the formidable Ladies' Aid Society.

She proceeded to list some urgent needs. "Mrs. Greggorio worries about a neighbor who looks like she's beaten regularly by her husband. If I had the where-with-all, I'd give her a train ticket back to her folks. But maybe she wouldn't go. It's hard to know."

Wanda grimaced and nodded like she might know the woman.

"I know another who's been sick since her baby was born," Miss Graves said. "She has no other children, but we worry she can't take care of even one."

The faces in our circle turned serious. It was going to be hard, knowing about more needs than we could help.

"From the tales the children tell at school, I believe there are mothers in all the mining towns who may be unskilled in hygiene and home-making. I once suggested that the Ladies' Aid give talks and demonstrations, but they're kind of stuck in their ways. Mostly what they do at their meetings is recite poems, read scripture and serve cake. They're good-hearted, but tradition decides their agenda, and no one is bold enough to suggest a change."

"Except you," Glory said.

Miss Graves smiled. "And I gave up."

"It's a good idea," Glory said. "We could sponsor informative programs and social gatherings for all the women, Methodist and Catholic alike. We'd need games or something to occupy their kids."

We agreed we did not want the membership of the welfare committee to be known and that we should not discuss people's needs with anyone not on the committee. "We can send word to each other if there's a reason to meet," Miss Graves said. "But you know, the assistance we give will only be a drop in the bucket. Most of the time we'll feel bad because we can't do more."

"The fact that we can't help everybody shouldn't stop us," Glory said. "Any little thing will help."

❦

AS ETTA KARAKAS HAD SAID, THERE WAS SOMETHING GOING around, and everyone feared it was the same disease that had killed our soldier.

Barlow brought home the *West Virginian* every evening, a newspaper published in Fairmont and delivered to the store by train. Not many families could afford the newspaper, but Will always tacked each day's pages to a bulletin board in the store. These days I seldom looked at the front page, which was full of war details, notices of union meetings and articles dedicated to the supply of rail cars, but in the issue dated September 24, one headline stood out. A town in Massachusetts had reported 5,000 cases of a deadly disease called Spanish Influenza.

"Some kids got sent home sick today," Evie said when she came the next afternoon for Otis.

Luzanna and I agreed it was likely no more than what had sickened the Karakas children, but I knew that like me, she was holding her breath.

I'd worried about Etta and her children, so I was relieved the next morning when she knocked on my front door. "Mrs. Townsend! Good, I got the right house."

"Mrs. Karakas, you're looking well!"

"We're good as can be." She smiled toward her children, all three sitting in the wagon. "I come to thank you for the wagon, it's a powerful gift. We're on our way to see about that cleaning job. Mrs. Herff said she'd meet us there."

"I'm sure she'd like you to call her Wanda," I said.

"That's what she said, but...you know."

"Whatever feels right to you. I hope you will call me May Rose."

"I'll try."

"Wanda may have told you, the men who live in the house where you're going—they're shy of people. Just do your best and don't be surprised or hurt if they don't take any notice of you or your work."

"She said they wouldn't be there."

"That's probably true. Wanda knows them well; just follow her suggestions about what you should do."

"This means so much. And the Mother's Pension? Mr. Townsend is helping me with the papers. All of us is grateful."

It felt good to have accomplished one helpful thing.

Simpson came to our door at the end of the day, returning one of my pie plates and bringing a gift of newly ground cornmeal. "We thank you for that meat pie. I'm not much of a cook, and Blanche...anyway, Blanche is happier these days, I think because you've introduced her to some folks. And she talks a lot about Charlie. I can't help wishing she'd settle down with a good man like him. Even though..."

"Oh, I don't think Charlie's likely to marry," I said, hoping my panic didn't show.

At dusk I heard more news of Blanche and Charlie when Russell appeared in the shadows of our porch. "Get that woman outa my house."

I stood in the doorway, holding Freddy. "Come in, please."

"Not coming in, I gotta get home. Tell her to get out."

"You mean Mrs. Karakas? You agreed to let her clean and do your laundry."

"I don't mean that'n. The other."

Now I understood. "Simpson's daughter?"

"Her's the one. Sitting in my house right now. Bothering Charlie."

I didn't want to tattle to Simpson. "Tell Charlie it's up to him to make her leave. I think he'll do what you say. Tomorrow Wanda and I will see what we can do." At present I couldn't think of anything short of telling Charlie and Russell to lock her out.

I relayed this problem the next morning when Wanda arrived with Otis. "Just yesterday Simpson said he hoped Blanche would settle down with a good man like Charlie, even though..."

"Settle down...even though? Did he say *even though*? What's that supposed to mean? Even though Charlie isn't quite right? Charlie does a good job and doesn't bother anyone. Blanche is the one who's a peck short of a bushel. Can you imagine her and Charlie...together?"

"Simpson said Charlie was a good man. We don't know, maybe Charlie likes her. Maybe he could steady her."

"Blanche is like a bitch in heat, Ma, pardon my language. You should of heard how Raz Cotton talked about her, his own wife, mother of his kids. And even if her and Charlie turned out to be good for each other, what if there was more babies? Aunt Piney don't need no more to care for."

I hadn't thought of babies, but I was starting to feel sorry for Blanche. "Maybe she can't have other children. She had no more in the three years she was away."

"And maybe she had 'em and forgot about 'em," Wanda said. "Left 'em somewhere."

"Surely not. I mean I hope not. Do you think Will might talk with Charlie? A man's the best choice, wouldn't you say, and Will's not only his brother, he's a doctor."

"Charlie and Will don't talk much. He's more likely to listen to me or Russell."

"You couldn't have a talk like that with Charlie."

"Not about what gets babies, 'cause I bet my bonnet he hasn't forgot that. But for sure I'm gonna tell him how she tied me up when Raz and Coyne kidnapped me. And how they left me to die up at the whiskey cave. I might tell him how she's been with a lot of men, though I figure Virgie's been with several, and she's got an eye for Charlie, too. Virgie would be better for Charlie."

"Wanda. Virgie? You can't be serious."

"Serious as fire hates water, but don't worry. Virgie won't go after him 'cause it might be upsetting to Glory and the rest of us. And she'd never settle down—he'd just be someone to fool with."

"Virgie would have such an unfair advantage over Charlie."

Wanda laughed. "Ma, when it comes to men, women always have the advantage. They just don't always know it."

The next day Wanda's news was not about Charlie and Blanche, but that every other person had a cold. The day after that she said the colds had turned into influenza, with fever, aches and pains. By evening she brought a worse report: a woman in Barbara Town had died, delirious with pain, wracked by coughing and bleeding from her nose and ears. And yes, her face had turned dark. Blue and purple, her family said.

I began to watch Freddy and Otis for the smallest sign of a sniffle.

At the end of the week, Wanda breathlessly reported the death of a miner at Big Bend. "Fine one day and dead the next. They say he was like our soldier, he had a cold. Next they knew he was coughing blood and turning purple."

She paused with a look of a child who needed assurance that the sky wasn't falling. I was speechless.

"So that makes one here," she said. "One at Barbara Town, and one at Big Bend. Folks at the store are talking of nothing but."

Whenever I heard of a spreading disease, my stomach sickened and I noticed new aches and pains. I supposed others reacted that way too. I'd learned to disregard my own symptoms. If I was really coming down with something, I'd know soon enough. But none of us had the leisure to take to our beds until it was impossible to keep going, no matter how thick our heads and how much we blew and coughed. Especially not mothers.

CHAPTER 9

I tried not to react to the rumors Wanda gathered from frightened customers. Barlow agreed there was too much exaggeration and false fear, but even he knew that in other places this terrible influenza was widespread. On October seventh, the *West Virginian* reported closure of schools and the ban of all public gatherings.

When she wasn't helping Will, Wanda was working in the store, because one of the new clerks had taken sick. A salesman there showed her a newspaper story about a prison where almost half of the sick had died. "The prisoners' faces turned black and they coughed up blood," she said. "Just like here."

Though I had my own fears, I tried to moderate her judgments. "I'm sure the spread and violence of disease is different in a prison where there is not strict cleanliness. Maybe the prisoners did not have good doctor care."

"Ma, doctors don't know anything about this. Dr. Pringle at Barbara Town said he couldn't do nothing but prescribe aspirin and cool sponge baths. Which didn't help that poor woman one bit."

"Did Will agree?"

"The family told it. These days Will don't hardly stop work to say hello."

So far none of us had the first sign of a cold, but in spite of my brave words, I felt like fire was about to rage from house to house. Will might easily bring the disease home to his family, and from there it could quickly spread to mine.

"What about masks? Does Will wear one when he treats his patients? I saw a newspaper photograph of war doctors and nurses wearing masks."

"Will says if people see a mask they'll think they're dying. He's been around a lot of sickness, and never catches anything. He's careful, Ma. He's forever washing his hands, and he puts on a clean white shirt every morning. It drives me crazy because I can't hardly keep up with his laundry. And he shaves every day. He says beards are unsanitary."

"But I'm sure you don't want him picking up Otis after he's been in a sick house. Aren't you worried?"

Wanda shrugged. "A little."

"And there you are in the store, and Alma too, face to face with all kinds. If people are dying, we should take every precaution."

"Only three people," she said.

In those few moments we'd switched positions. "Half the sick died in that prison, your words, Wanda. If I make masks, will you and Will wear them?"

"Most folks has just got the small flu. Masks are gonna make them really scared."

"Maybe they should be," I said. "Maybe we all should be."

We were diverted by the sound of our children's laughter. Otis was clutching the bars of the baby pen, rocking himself back and forth. On the other side of the bars, Freddy sat and waved his arms.

"Okay, if you make a mask, I'll try it. And you can ease your mind about one other thing—I gave Charlie the nasty truth about

Blanche."

"I hope not too nasty. How do you think he took it?"

"You know Charlie seldom says three words together, so it's hard to tell. But he knew who I was talking about. I got no idea if he welcomes her or thinks she's a pest. What do you think, should we tell Virgie to go after him?"

"Please don't say anything to Virgie. Let's wait and see what happens. Maybe this will all work out for the best."

After she left with Otis, I carried a lantern upstairs to one of our unfinished rooms where there was a chest full of sheets we'd bought for beds still unassembled. If invisible germs were floating on the air, the tightly-woven sheets might make better masks than my other option, a bolt of white flannel. I brought two sheets to the kitchen but delayed cutting, hoping Barlow would come home and say all the sick were recovering.

I was watching for Barlow at the front door when I heard Luzanna call my name. The shrillness of her tone made me hurry to the kitchen. I expected to see her in the doorway, but she stood in the middle of the back yard.

I called, "Luzanna! Why are you out here?" But I knew.

"Tim and Emmy's got the flu," she said. "I won't come in, but if you put your laundry on the porch tomorrow, I'll do it."

I didn't want her to see my panic, no more than I wanted to feel it. I'd known Emmy and Tim to be sick in other seasons. "Take care of your kids; I can wash our clothes."

"May Rose, I gotta have work."

"We'll pay you same as always and you can catch up later. Write down what you need from the store and I'll have Barlow bring it home. Is Alma well?"

"Yes. She's with the kids now. Will is gonna come to the house soon as he can."

Now it was here, the wildfire I could not wish away. "Are Tim and Emmy badly sick? How do they feel?"

"Same as every other time they've had the flu. They'll be okay tomorrow or the next day." It was what she had to believe.

"I'm sure they will." It was the assurance I had to give. "I'll bring your supper and leave it on your porch." Feeding those who were well wasn't as good as helping at the bedside of the sick, but she understood. Because of my family, it was my only choice.

❦

BARLOW DID NOT COME HOME WITH GOOD NEWS. "MY DEAR, I don't want you to get upset if you hear someone say it's the plague." He stopped in the kitchen doorway.

"The plague! Barlow!"

"Will says it's not the plague. But it's spreading fast and people say it's terrible."

"How terrible?" I could not stop thinking of faces turning blue, purple, and black.

"A child died, one of the Findlay family."

"Oh, Barlow, a child!"

Freddy cried a loud "Umm" and stretched his arms to his father.

Like Freddy, I wanted the comfort of Barlow's arms, but he did not move from the threshold, and he stopped my steps with a raised hand.

"Barlow! Are you sick?"

"No, I'm fine. Will said the child's illness was like the others. She was healthy two days ago, then developed a fever and that awful coughing."

"And the dark face?"

"Blotches, yes."

"The poor mother."

"Every member of that family is sick."

"*No.* Barlow, Luzanna's children are sick."

"I heard. We need to keep our heads and do what we can. Will has put signs on the school, the church and the store. Don't go to public places like the school or church or even the store unless it's an emergency. Don't drink from someone else's cup, or eat with their utensils unless they've been boiled. Keep a handkerchief over the mouth when sneezing or coughing. Boil handkerchiefs. Boil all soiled clothes."

I was already practicing most of those measures. I could not bear the thought of the worst happening to Emmy and Tim. Mrs. Karakas and her children had gotten well in just a day, and at present there seemed no way to know if Emmy and Tim had the small flu or the kind that had killed the Findlay child.

Freddy was now squealing for Barlow's attention, so I lifted and carried him to the other side of the room. I had been boiling beef for supper, thinking Luzanna's children might take sips of broth once they felt better, and the meat would help keep up her strength. To keep from crying, I pushed a masher up and down in a large pot of potatoes.

"The preacher is upset about closing the church," Barlow said. "In his opinion we should be there on our knees at least once a day."

I rapped the potato masher against the side of the pot. "He must be an idiot. Everyone can safely go to their knees at home, and their prayers will be heard just the same. But what about the mine and the store? Will you close them?"

"We haven't decided."

"And what about Will? Isn't he afraid of carrying the flu home to his family?"

"I don't know. What about me?"

"Barlow! Are you sure you're well?"

"I'm fine. I mean I could carry the disease home, too. As far as I know, most of our miners are well and they want to keep working. Remember, a lot of people have been sick, but only four have died. We need to take precautions, that's all."

Freddy squirmed in my arms. "Stay home with us," I said. "A

few days, until this passes."

"I can't. But I want to keep you and Freddy safe. I'll sleep in my office until this is over."

The thought of being without him was enough to make me sick. I wanted to say he'd promised never to leave me. That he owed it to us to stay here and keep himself safe. That four had died, one a child. That he was almost 55 years old and perhaps should take greater care. "Please," I said.

"May Rose, there's so much to do, and I may already be exposed. You too. Will says there are families where everyone has the flu and no one to care for them. He wants to move those cases into the church. Wanda and some of the parents of sick children are going to help. I'll be helping Mr. Wise keep the store open until... I think we need to keep the store open as long as possible. People will need food and other things."

All of this was so strange—I needed to hear it again and again to take it in. "Wanda is going to expose herself to that disease? What about Evie and Otis?"

He bent his head and did not look up for such a long time that I thought he was either angry with me or struggling not to cry.

"Barlow." I could not imagine staying away if he needed me.

"Each family will have to decide for itself. I'm deciding to keep you and Freddy safe. Will has no choice—he won't shirk his duty—but in my opinion Wanda should protect her children. I'll put a cot in my office."

"No. I need you here. We need you." The walls of the two rooms at the front of the house were still un-plastered, but they had doors and windows and access to the hall bathroom, and in one of them was the bed we'd set up for Otis and Evie.

"Come into the house through the front door and sleep in the front room," I said. "I'll feel better, knowing you're under this roof. We can talk through the wall." Morning and night, I'd hear him say he was well.

Barlow was always slow to decide. His gaze moved everywhere

as he considered—toward the floor, the ceiling, and absently around the kitchen. At last he looked at me. "All right, but if I sneeze even once, I'll move to my office."

"I'm going to sew masks. I told Wanda I'd make them for her and Will. I want you to wear one too."

He smiled. "A mask? I suppose I can wear one, if I have to be near someone who is sick. But otherwise...I don't know."

I was seldom angry with Barlow, but I was angry now. "Remember, you said we can be exposed without knowing it. Please, wear the mask." I watched him step off the back porch, then I heard the front door close and the sound of cartons shoved across the wooden floor. "Barlow?"

When he answered, I said, "I'm taking supper to Luzanna. I'll have to leave Freddy in the baby pen. He'll be fine."

"What if he cries?"

"If he cries, he cries. It won't hurt him."

I carried a pot of potatoes in one hand and one of boiled beef in the other. Dry leaves flew along the ground, and overhead the sky had turned flat and gray. I hurried downhill toward Luzanna's house with my sweaty neck turning cold and my skirt billowing around my ankles.

I knocked on Luzanna's back door and left the pots on the porch. When a window opened above and Luzanna called her thanks, I waved and left, feeling cowardly. A week or two at most, I thought. In a week or two, the flu would die out. We could rearrange our lives for a week or two.

The room where Barlow, Freddy and I slept was beside the kitchen. Someday it was to be our dining room, but for now our bed was pushed against the door to the unfinished parlor where Barlow would sleep for a few nights. During this time of separation, he and I could talk through the wall. At other times he would stand in the yard where I could see him and say good morning or good night. I would hold Freddy for him to see.

Freddy was sobbing tears of abandonment when I returned to

the kitchen. He lifted his arms and I took him to my rocking chair and opened my dress to let him nurse. Even after he began to suck, he stopped at times to gasp and choke. I stroked his bald head. No one would dispute that he was my most important concern, but because of him, I could be no comfort to my husband. And I would miss him.

Barlow rapped on the wall and called, "May Rose, are you there? I'm going to ask Charlie to help me carry down a chest of drawers."

"Be careful," I said, meaning *keep your distance from Charlie.* It was like a split had opened in the earth, forcing me away from everyone I loved.

Later I heard the sound of men's voices and the thump of feet up and down the stairs. That night I put Freddy to bed in the kitchen's baby pen so he would not be disturbed when I talked to Barlow through the wall of his new sleeping room.

I set a chair close to the wall. "Barlow. Is this going to work?"

"We'll make it work. You were right; I'd miss you more if I were in my office."

"Maybe we don't need to sleep apart. Maybe it's a foolish caution."

"We don't know. We can try for a few days."

"You sound far away. Are you in bed?"

"Yes, sitting up. Thinking of you."

Barlow did not often say how he felt, and at times I thought he hesitated to show affection, as though afraid I'd laugh at his attempts or shrug him away. It was unusual to hear him say he was thinking of me.

"I've always been proud of you," I said. "How you listened to Hester's opinions and allowed her to run the boardinghouse. And when I worked at the lumber company, I admired you more because I could see how the employees respected you." I felt like we were saying goodbye.

"We were separated too many years," he said.

"I'm glad Wanda and Will have been working together. I'd like to work where I could see and hear you all the time."

"If so, you might discover my worst. But if you stick with me I'll have a chance to be better."

"I'll be sticking. You be sure to stick with us."

Since Freddy's birth, I'd worried like never before that some accident or illness would take Barlow from us. He yawned, and I heard the bed creak. I imagined him standing up and undressing. I thought of helping him off with his suspenders, running my hands from his shoulders to his waist, which always made him turn to kiss me. I pushed away a new thought of him lying in bed, coughing blood.

We said goodnight. Back in the kitchen I folded and cut a sheet into rectangles. Then I hummed while I hemmed and stitched, silently naming each of my family and friends, as though the intensity of my thoughts would protect them. I'd seen too much to believe that God would keep us from all harm, but I knew it was important to keep saying and singing those words. When overcome by bad reports, we needed hope.

CHAPTER 10

I bolted upright in bed, shocked awake by a boom of cannon and a vision of Wanda and Will against a fiery sky, about to be overcome by soldiers in spiked helmets, charging with swords and bayonets. Another explosion of light and sound brightened the room. I spoke aloud: "Please, not the mine." Then thunder shook the house, and I released my breath and pulled up the blanket at the foot of the bed. It was only a storm. The air was cold.

"Barlow," I whispered. Thunder usually woke us all, but I heard no responding word and no cry from Freddy. I pressed an ear to the wall until I detected a shift of bedsprings.

The kitchen was slightly warmer, but Freddy had rolled from under his blanket and now lay sleeping on his stomach with his nightdress tangled around his waist and his fat legs bare. I pulled the blanket over him, then gently opened the firebox and slid a chunk of wood on the coals. Someday our house was to be heated by a furnace in the basement. Pipes wrapped in sheets of asbestos were already in the walls, ready to carry heat to every room, but like so much else, the furnace waited to be assembled.

I'd gone to bed late after cutting twenty masks and stitching ten, worrying with every needle's punch, mainly about Luzanna and her children. Now I carried the cut pieces to my bed, closed the door to the kitchen and pulled the string that turned on the electric bulb.

I finished two masks before Freddy woke and fussed for his breakfast. I diapered him and felt his forehead to be sure he was well. At this moment, mothers everywhere must be worrying the same thoughts, holding their infants to their breasts and testing their foreheads for fever.

After Freddy nursed his fill, I carried him around the room while I put water and coffee in the percolator and set it on the stove to boil. He was getting harder to hold on one arm, so I set him in the baby pen while I cut squares of cornmeal mush. Then I knocked on Barlow's wall.

"I'm awake," he said.

I needed to see his face. "Did you sleep well?" Meaning *tell me you're all right*.

"Very well. And you?" He sounded formal, as though the wall had made us strangers.

"We're well," I said.

"Good."

"This will pass. It always does. We've just not been through something like this before."

"I'm sure you're right."

"Maybe in a few days. And this is better than staying in your office, isn't it?"

"Much better."

"And you feel fine?"

"I do."

"If you were sleeping in your office, I wouldn't know about you."

"I know. Do I hear rain?"

"It's been raining, yes."

"What do I hear?"

It was not yet light, but at the kitchen door, someone was knocking who could not wait for the sun to come up nor the rain to stop. I was afraid it was Luzanna. Coming so early, it could not be good news.

"I'll set your breakfast in the hall," I said, hurrying to the kitchen door. As I opened it, Wanda backed to the edge of the porch, holding a slicker over her head.

"I'm not bringing Otis today." She shouted over the rain hammering the porch's tin roof.

"Good Lord. He's not sick?"

"He's fine, rotten as usual. We're going to quarantine him and Evie for a couple of days to be sure they're healthy, then..."

"Wanda?"

"Then we'd like to give both of them to you to keep...as long as this lasts."

Wind sprayed a cold mist of rain through the open door. I clutched my arms to my middle. "You and Will...Wanda, are you well?"

"We're fine." She sounded exhausted. "Tell Barlow to stay home."

"I tried. He says he must help in the store. He's sleeping in a front room and won't come into the same room with us. Yes, of course Otis and Evie may stay with me." I struggled between wanting to hug her and needing her to keep away.

Wanda shifted her feet, rustling leaves that had blown onto the porch. "Ma, a young woman died an hour ago, Mrs. Karakas."

"Etta!"

"Not that one. Her sister-in-law."

"*No*. That pretty girl?"

"I know."

"Her name was Marie." This death struck closer than the others. I'd seen her with her children; I knew something of her troubles. "And the rest of the family?"

"Not sick. Yet."

"She had four small children."

"I know. I was there at the end. It was bad."

I did not want to know how bad, and for once, Wanda seemed unwilling to pass along the details. "Will said to ask the committee to give the family something from the welfare fund," she said. "The Findlay family too."

"I'll do that," I said. "It's fortunate, isn't it, that we've already organized to give aid." As soon as I spoke I wanted to take back those words. There was nothing fortunate about this situation, but in difficult times we did not always act and speak rationally.

"Will hasn't slept in days. I can't let him do this alone." She sounded desperate.

"Tell Will I'm proud of what he's doing. You too. You and Will, your children—and Charlie—you're as precious to me as Freddy."

"We know."

"If it helps, send Otis with Evie this morning. I'll isolate them in one of the front rooms. Barlow is keeping himself to the other."

"I think we'll just go ahead and wait three days. Otis won't be happy confined to one room, so it will be easier for Evie if we do that at home. And if they get sick, I'll be right there. Will too." She took a deep breath. "So three days from now—that will be Friday—Evie will bring him. If they don't come..."

I took my stack of masks from the table. "All right, three days. I made masks for you."

She kept her place at the edge of the porch. "Don't come close."

I bundled the masks and tossed them to her through the door. My heart thumped as I thought of the sickrooms where she'd been and the others where she would follow her husband. "Wanda, I need to know you're okay, every day. And please send for me if you're not."

"I don't want you to come if I'm sick. I want you to stay right here and take care of my kids."

"I will. You know I will."

"There's something else. Ma, this isn't... it isn't good. Will says... last night... last night..."

My breath slowed as she faltered.

"Emmy and Tim... Will says... they may not make it."

When she finished I lost control, gripped the railing of the baby pen and sobbed. I'd taught Emmy and Tim to add and subtract. I'd joined in their games. Luzanna had nearly killed herself, trying to find them a home.

Freddy whimpered. I wiped my eyes on my sleeve. "What can I do?"

"You can't help them now. *Keep our kids.* Keep them safe."

Barlow pounded on the wall. "May Rose, are you and the baby all right?"

I lifted Freddy and wrapped the blanket around him. "Perfect." My voice came out too high and chirpy.

"Friday," Wanda said.

Her image dissolved in the dark, and I closed the door and returned Freddy to his pen. He'd become such a good baby, and now I kept setting him aside. Wiping my eyes with my sleeve, I began to fry the mush for Barlow's breakfast.

When I set Barlow's plate at the door to his room, I reported Wanda's news. "She says you should stay home. She says the sickness is bad."

Again he did not speak for a few moments, and it took all my strength not to open his door. "I feel as bad as you do about Luzanna's children," he said at last. "There's a prayer list tacked to the church door. I'll add their names."

"Barlow, we need more than prayer. Wear a mask in the store, I don't care if you feel foolish. You'll be close to people who may be getting sick and to others who've been exposed, like Wanda and Will. If you wear a mask, they may follow your example. Do it for us. Do it for everyone."

The rain ended, and I set masks and breakfast outside for Barlow to carry to Luzanna's porch, along with the remainder of the fried mush and bacon for Wanda and Will.

All morning I sewed and baked, afraid for Wanda and fueled by guilt that I was keeping myself safe while my family and friends battled an enemy they could not identify until it was too late. When Freddy fussed in the baby pen, I sat him in the buggy and jiggled it with my foot while I mixed and kneaded bread dough. When he tired of the buggy, I returned him to the baby pen and bent the handles of two spoons so he could safely hold and strike them together. When he cried to be picked up, I sang hymns, and he stopped crying and listened, perhaps struck by the odd sounds, for as much as I loved to sing, my voice could never find the right tune. I tried not to think of four people dead, one a child. Of everyone sick in the Findlay house. Of Marie Karakas. I could not stop thinking about Luzanna's children. They had to get well.

In ordinary times, I would not have left Freddy alone, but late in the morning I put on a sweater and a mask and delivered two loaves of bread to Luzanna's porch. When I returned, Charlie stood beside his horse at our garden gate.

"We're not sick," I called. "Are you and Russell all right?"

He nodded. Even from a distance I could see he was trying to say something.

"Wanda," he said.

I held my breath. "Is she sick?"

"Wants..." He rotated his hand, like he was trying to find the word. He tugged the cloth of his trousers. "Baby...pants."

"Diapers?"

"Diapers." He held out his arms.

"Wait here." Last winter, Luzanna and I had hemmed four dozen squares of flannel for diapers. Most of these were clean; the ones from yesterday were soaking in a pail on the porch. I hurried inside and returned with a stack of folded diapers, a bunch of safety pins, and a loaf of bread wrapped in newspaper. "The bread is for you and Russell."

Charlie motioned to the table by our sugar maple, and stood back while I set everything there.

"Thank you for doing this," I said.

He said nothing, just turned and walked away with the supplies, followed by his horse.

Barlow had said he would not come home for lunch. I ate a heel of bread and nursed Freddy, and while he slept, washed his diapers and thought about what I could cook to feed a lot of people. I had a salty shank end of ham, and in our basement, cabbage, onions, carrots and potatoes. After pinning the diapers to the clothesline, I brought down my bolt of diaper flannel and began to cut.

In the afternoon, Charlie and Russell appeared in the back yard with a message that Wanda wanted my washing machine. I motioned to where it sat on the porch, then watched from the house as they carried it to their wagon and hauled it away.

It was dark when I heard Barlow's step on the porch, then his voice. "May Rose, how are you?"

I opened the kitchen door. "We're fine. Raise your lantern so I can see your face."

The lantern lit one side of his face and shadowed the other, revealing half of his thin smile.

He lifted the mask that hung from strings around his neck. "See? I wore it all day. And I'm well, just tired. There were no new deaths in Winkler today. I suppose this is not encouraging, but we're not alone—the newspaper says this disease is marching across the country."

The idea of everyone sick was the opposite of encouragement. The only thing that kept me from panic was to keep my hands busy in some helpful way.

"People were glad to get your masks," he said.

"Good, and bless you for wearing yours. I'm making more, and I've made enough stew for a dozen people. Do you know who might need it?"

"Many. I'll take it to the church. Can we spare blankets?"

We had bedding that had never been used. I filled the buggy with quilts, blankets, bowls and spoons and my large pot of stew, then pushed it through the doorway.

"We may get none of this back," he said.

"It doesn't matter. I'll cook again tomorrow." I felt encouraged because he hadn't said anything about Emmy and Tim. "Have you heard anything about Luzanna's children? Or the Karakas family?"

"Nothing today."

"Soon all this will be over."

"We'll be fine," he said. He wheeled the buggy away, and I hurried to Luzanna's with a smaller pot of stew. From her porch I heard the sad moans of a child. I'd been breathing fast, but now my breath slowed to the rhythm of those moans.

Alma opened the door. "Emmy and Tim are the same. And now Ma is sick," she said.

"Oh, sweetheart. Tell me what to do."

"Ma doesn't want you to catch this. I can take care of them." She lifted the pot of stew. "This will help me. The others too, if they get well enough to eat. Doc Will said he'd come tonight."

I stumbled home. Every minute seemed to bring a new worry until the hours were weighed with fear.

BARLOW AND I DID NOT TRY TO TALK AGAIN UNTIL AFTER I PUT Freddy to bed in the kitchen. Then I closed the door to the kitchen and knocked on the wall between us. After we assured ourselves that we were well, I said, "Tell me what Wanda and Will are doing. How do they seem?"

"They're called out a lot and they see people in Will's treatment room. They don't come into the store. Charlie is helping them."

"No. Not Charlie too."

"I don't think they asked, he just appeared. He helped carry sick people to the church. I saw him at a campfire on the track side of the street. I think some of the miners are sleeping out, the ones with sickness at home."

"Barlow, Luzanna is sick," I said.

"I know. I'm sorry."

Luzanna had attended Freddy's birth and stayed with me in the days after, easing my fears. "I should be with her."

"Freddy," he said.

"I know, I know."

"Will said Emmy and Tim are hanging on. He says it's a good sign. They have bad coughs, but have not spit up blood."

"Poor Alma is trying to take care of them all."

"It's the same in many homes. Wanda helped Alma for a few hours today, cleaning up, that kind of thing."

"I'm glad she can help and I wish she wouldn't, isn't that terrible? And why did she send Charlie and Russell for my washing machine?"

"They put her machine and ours on the store's loading dock for anyone to use."

It was a fine idea. Our machines had electric motors and wringers. From the activity I'd seen in back yards on washdays, I believed most women in Winkler had only washtubs and washboards.

"Charlie ran a temporary water line to the dock," Barlow said, "and the store is supplying chlorine bleach. You may smell fires—I hear some of the bedding from the sick is so fouled that no one wants to wash it. I can get a new machine for you in a few days."

"That's thoughtful, thank you." Losing the washing machine didn't matter. I was afraid I would lose everyone.

CHAPTER 11

I rose early the next morning, hoping Wanda would appear and prove she was well. But she did not come, and once again Barlow left for work carrying breakfast to her and to Alma. The morning was warm and breezy, a good day for drying clothes on the line. While Freddy napped, I scrubbed his diapers on a washboard, then boiled them on the stove. As I wrung them out, I worried about Etta Karakas, who if she wasn't sick by now, must be washing diapers twice each day and spending hours changing and feeding the extra children in her charge. If she had something to feed them. I hoped someone would tell her about the washing machines on the store's loading docks.

While Freddy napped, I dumped our trash in the burn barrel at the far edge of our yard, but did not light it because of the wind and the probability that smoke would scent and soil my clean diapers.

I wasn't expecting to see anyone and hadn't heard anyone approach, but when I turned to go to the house, I bumped into Blanche Cotton, who'd crept up close behind me. Perhaps it was only surprise that made me think her bright eyes and wide smile had a look of madness. I dodged and ran toward the house, waving my arms to warn her away.

"I'm not gonna hurt you," she called.

I stopped at my screen door. "Please step back and keep your distance. The sickness."

"Are you sick?"

"No, Blanche. I'm trying to stay away from people. You should do that too—go home and confine yourself to the house."

She stopped at the clothesline and touched one of the diapers flapping in the wind. "These are dry. Want me to take them down and fold them for you?"

"No, thank you."

She unpinned a diaper and folded it on the table. "I could help. I done this a lot. I had three babies."

"Please, go home. This sickness is bad."

"I don't have anyone to talk to. Miss Virgie and Miss Glory are talking to everybody. They're walking all over town, stopping at every house. They chased me away."

"It's for your own good," I said. "They don't want you to get sick or carry the disease to other people."

"When folks open their doors, Miss Virgie asks about the sick in the house and Miss Glory writes on paper," Blanche said. "I could do that."

"They're finding out if people need help." I assumed it was so.

"Can I come in?"

"No. I have to protect my baby."

"I'd never hurt him."

"I mean protect him from the disease. I don't let anyone in."

"Not even Wanda?"

"Not even her. And I don't go anywhere or get close to anyone, not even my husband. Go home, Blanche. The town is full of influenza. People have died—it's very bad."

"I saw a man puke in the street."

"See? If you're out and about you could spread the disease."

"Wanda is out and about. Miss Virgie and Miss Glory are out and about."

"They're helping. Someone has to help. Some of us have to stay well at home."

"It's lonely at home, with Piney and my babies gone. I could help Wanda, but she don't like me. And now Charlie don't like me neither."

"Then go to the mill and help your father."

"The school closed up and he took Ruby to wherever Piney is. He wouldn't let me go." She touched a diaper again. "I could help you."

"Other people need help more than I do. Why not go to the store where they're washing clothes?"

"I washed clothes for my kids, but Piney don't let me do that now."

"Maybe she will when she comes back."

"I might go away to someplace else. My kids don't know me."

"Things will get better for you. Go home, or find a place that needs help. Do you have a mask like everyone's wearing?"

"No, ma'am."

"Wait right there." I brought four masks outside and set them on the table. "These are for you and your father. Wear one every day."

"If you say so."

I stood in my doorway and watched her leave. At the edge of the yard she stopped and called, "It's okay if Wanda don't like me. I'll come back and talk to you."

I closed my door against the putrid odor rising from the town's burn barrels. I was glad Blanche had not asked my opinion of how her life would get better, for she seemed unlikely to change.

ONCE AGAIN BARLOW DID NOT COME HOME FOR LUNCH. Mid-afternoon, I took the diapers from the line, then carried Freddy and a fresh loaf of bread to Luzanna's house. Crossing her yard, I saw a small boy rise from the porch and run the other direction, hugging to his chest the pot of oatmeal I'd sent that morning with Barlow.

I waited until the boy disappeared, then hurried to Luzanna's door, knocked and backed to the edge of the porch. After a time of silence, I went again and knocked louder and longer, backed away once more and waited, disturbed by visions of everyone in Luzanna's family sick, dying, or dead.

When no one came to the door. I stood in her yard and looked at the upstairs window where she'd called to me a few days ago. No smoke came from Luzanna's chimney. In the entire quiet town, only the beat of mine ventilation fans and smoke rising from the trash fires gave evidence that anyone else was alive.

I left Luzanna's bread on her porch, and when I got home, set another loaf on the table in our back yard. The boy who'd carried off my pot of oatmeal might have parents who were sick or worse. He might be feeding smaller brothers and sisters. I kept looking through the window to check on that loaf while I cared for Freddy, cooked another stew and stitched diapers and masks. The meat in the stew was tender by the time Barlow was due for our evening meal, but he did not come home, and neither Russell nor Charlie came to take the stew to those at the church.

The last time there was enough daylight to see my yard, I realized the loaf was no longer on the table. I hoped Virgie and Glory would learn about the boy's family.

I carried Freddy and a small pot of stew to Luzanna's porch by the glow of the harvest moon. There was no light inside the house, but I could see the new loaf was still there. This time I pounded on the kitchen door, and when I got no answer, did the same at the front. Alma opened the upstairs window. "I'm sick," she said. "But Em and Tim are better, I think."

I was glad for them but now worried for poor Alma. "And your ma?"

"She feels pretty bad."

Alma disappeared, leaving the window open. I waited for her to return, and when she did not, I called her name. Emmy appeared at the open window. "Alma's puking," she said.

"Emmy, tell me what I can do to help."

"Have you got aspirin? We used up all Doc left. Ma says maybe when she and Alma stops puking they'll be able to keep it down."

I returned home, set Freddy in the baby pen, dashed back alone and set our bottle of aspirin by Luzanna's back door.

At home again, I picked a potato and piece of carrot from the stew and mashed them fine, then set Freddy on my lap and while he waved his arms and tried to get his hands in the plate, I recited nursery rhymes and fed him small bites of his first solid food. In a time when everything seemed to be falling to ruin, my child provided essential moments of joy.

Later I sat at the table and sewed, puncturing my wash-reddened thumb with repeated stabs of the needle through layers of strong cloth, rising too often to go to the front porch to see if Barlow was coming up the street. The night was clear and quiet, and though it was warm enough for open windows and evening strolls and there were lights in many houses, I saw no moving shadows on the streets below and heard no more than an occasional closing of a door and bits of muted conversation. Luzanna and Barlow were constantly on my mind, along with Wanda and Will, who were on the front lines of this war. I needed to be assured about all of them, and I needed to see Barlow soon.

I was asleep, sitting fully dressed in bed, when the mine whistle shrilled. It was not the signal for the start of a shift but the ear-splitting notice of an accident. In the next minutes, I gathered what information I could from a solitary vigil on the front porch: the slam of doors, padding of running feet, wind-blown words. In house after house, lights came on, then for a long time after that there were no sounds other than the drone of crickets. I slumped on the front steps and cried.

The moon had reached its height before I heard the clop of a horse's hooves and saw a dark rider coming my way. Charlie.

"Accident at the mine," he said.

I held onto a roof post to keep from spilling to the floor. Barlow seldom went down into the mine, but I thought of him first. "Barlow? Will?"

"Last I saw they was at the portal."

For a single moment, I felt joyous, because they were safe. But some were not, and everyone in town might collapse under the strain of so much misfortune. I waited to hear.

"Man was smoking and picked up a stick of dynamite. He was outside."

An explosion outside seemed better than underground. "Is he dead?"

"Nah. Looks like it tore off his arm. Will and that other doctor is with him."

For Charlie, this was an extended conversation. He could not tell me the man's name or if he had a family.

"Thank you for coming. Did Barlow send a message?"

"Just to tell you...something. Maybe that was it."

"I have a pot of stew for people at the church," I said.

"Okay."

"Have you seen Wanda?"

"At the church."

"She's well?"

"Keeps me hauling water." He lifted a mask tied around his neck. "Yells at me to wear this."

"Good, please do what she says. And Russell?"

"Went home."

"And Barlow was well, when you saw him last?"

"Seemed like."

Then I remembered everything else. "Charlie, tell Wanda that Alma is sick."

"Okay."

"If you see Barlow, tell him I'm out of flour." In view of so much distress, flour seemed unimportant, except that people who were taking care of others needed bread. "And ask him to bring home aspirin."

"It's a lot to remember," Charlie said.

"I'll write it down."

Charlie walked away with my list of requests, my last loaf of bread and all the stew except the bowl I'd set aside for Barlow.

Barlow came home late, empty handed and too tired to talk or eat. Before I dressed for bed, I covered a pot of dry beans with water. It was my last large pot. I'd have to tell someone to empty it and bring it back, otherwise I wouldn't be able to cook even for ourselves.

CHAPTER 12

I began my tasks the next morning with less sense of disruption. Our new arrangement was beginning to feel almost routine, evidence that we could adjust to anything—the absence of friends, an epidemic, even the loss of an arm. My morning prayer was that the day would bring no more death. I did not feel confident.

When at last Barlow responded to my knock on his wall, his speech was slow and tired. "I didn't bring your flour last night," he said.

I set his coffee and breakfast outside his door. "You worked far too late. If I give you a grocery order, can Charlie deliver it?"

"If you need very much, I can bring it in Randolph's automobile."

"Tomorrow is the day Evie and Otis are to come. I'm out of everything, and we'll need another bed brought downstairs."

"All right."

"Will the injured miner make a good recovery?"

"I think so. Will is to send him to a hospital today, by train."

"His name?"

"Adams. Young man, no family. He should've known better."

It was terrible but true that the man's responsibility for his accident probably made everyone feel less grief for his loss. Like so much else about myself, I was not proud of this feeling, but I did not think about it for long. With tragic events becoming our daily companions, there seemed no choice but to carry on, girding ourselves with prayer and protecting our sanity by trying to forget.

The best part of that morning was the arrival of Virgie and Glory, garbed not in their usual dresses of bright cloth with lace and embroidery, but in sober gray and brown. Today they were continuing their survey of every household.

They stood at a distance, asked about our health and made me feel infinitely better with the news that Luzanna and her family appeared to be recovering.

"Will says this disease can have a lingering effect," Glory said. "Luzanna may need our help for some time."

I admired their calm and sturdy demeanor, which must have been an encouragement to people in the homes they surveyed. "I wish I could do more."

"Nonsense," Virgie said. "You're feeding lots of people. When we stopped at Luzanna's, Emmy and Tim were eating your stew for breakfast."

"Have there been more deaths?" Barlow's answer to this question had been vague. I hoped that meant there were none.

"Four yesterday," Virgie said. "The undertaker can't keep up. And if there's funerals, I don't think anybody goes."

Glory read the names and identities of the most recent deaths. One miner, one child, an elderly parent, and a teacher, not Miss Graves, who'd gone home to her brother's farm. "Some people have a mild case, but in others, the disease is violent, awful to see and painful to bear."

"Please take care. Wear your masks."

"Glory makes me wear it," Virgie said. "Lots of women are

CAROL ERVIN

sewing masks now, if they ain't sick themselves, and I'm glad to say they're helping their neighbors as they can."

"And what of Wanda? Is she being careful?"

"I don't know how she can, 'cause she's in the thick of it," Virgie said. "And now Barlow's the only one in the store. That Mr. Wise and the new clerks has skipped town. With so many miners sick, Randolph said the mine's going down to one shift today."

"We'll keep the welfare committee informed of needs," Glory said. "We're asking people to tack notes on their doors if they need help. At present the Karakas family tops our list. Do you agree they should be the next to receive Winkler Welfare?"

For me it was an easy choice.

Before Virgie and Glory left, I said, "If you see Blanche, please suggest something she can do. I think she feels lost as a leaf in a windstorm."

Glory frowned. "That Blanche! She's flitting all over town, likely picking up germs and passing them along. We've told her again and again told she cannot accompany us. But the next time she gets within hearing distance, I'll try to direct her to something useful."

"I told her she might help with the washing at the store dock."

"That's miserable work," Virgie said. "We'll see how much she really wants to help."

Mid-morning, I nearly fainted with joy when Emmy and Tim came into my yard. They carried pots I'd left at their house, now crusty with dried bits of food.

"Ma said not to come in your house," Emmy said. "We might still be catching."

"But you're well! And Alma and your ma?"

Tim set a pot on the outside table. "They don't want to eat yet, but we do."

I sent them home with enough beans and cornbread for their mother and sister. My next visitor was Wanda, who tapped on my kitchen door. "You all good in there?"

"Not a sniffle. I'm relieved to see you. You're well?"

Her face looked years older, but she wore a new white apron and her hair was tucked under a spotless cap.

"So far."

I knew she was only being honest, given what she must be experiencing, but I was frightened by the lack of her usual confidence.

"We'll get through this," I said, brave words from one who hadn't seen anything to one who had seen the worst.

"Sure. I told Charlie to round up your cook pots."

"Bless you. I think Luzanna and Alma are recovering. Tim and Emmy were here this morning." I saw her shoulders lift and fall in a sigh. She swiped a hand over her eyes.

"So tomorrow is the day you'll bring Evie and Otis?"

"Looks that way. Gotta go." She left the yard with half a wave.

At noon, Charlie delivered my other cook pots and Barlow arrived with my grocery order in Randolph's automobile. Then Charlie returned with Russell and they set up a bed for Otis and Evie in the other front room. The rest of the day I saw no one. I was glad for ordinary sounds, the shift whistle, the chug of arriving and departing trains, and from the stock yards, the mooing of cattle. At times I heard nothing but the ticking of our grandfather clock. It was easy to think Freddy and I were the only living souls in town, for our kitchen and yard faced the wooded slope, and no traffic came to our street unless it was destined for our house. Often I went to the front porch to look over the town. The quiet roofs gave no suggestion of what might be happening beneath. I envied Wanda, Virgie and Glory, who knew what was going on, even if that knowledge was hard to bear. I also had moments of pity for Blanche. In dire situations, we all needed something to keep us from going crazy.

Before sundown, Barlow came home with a bad report—six more deaths in Winkler and five across the river in Barbara Town.

He sat at the table under the bare-limbed maple tree. I stood on the porch, stunned by the numbers, thinking of bereaved families and the reported horrors of the disease.

"May Rose," he said, "Will is on his way. We think you should take the children to Lucie Bosell's farm."

"To Lucie's? What's brought this change?" But I knew. Will and Wanda were exhausted and frightened, seeing so much, unable to stop the deaths. They must fear for themselves as well.

"Everything's ready here," I said, "and our house is quite isolated. We've been doing well, and things have to get better. Luzanna and her family are improving."

"I'm glad to hear it, but others are worse."

"I will be worse without you. If it makes Wanda and Will feel better, they can certainly send their children away. There's no room for Freddy and me at Lucie's, and no need for us to go. We'll stay here."

"What if I insist?" He sounded tired, not insistent.

"Barlow, are you afraid?"

He breathed heavily. "I am."

"Then stay home with us. Sleep in the other room if you must, or come back to me and we'll take whatever comes together." If I couldn't be with my husband and friends, I needed to see them from a distance and hear them speak. I needed to know Barlow was well, and I wanted to occupy myself in ways that let me think I was helping, even if my efforts did not cure anyone.

"May Rose, you know I can't stay home. There's no one else to tend the store and take care of business for the mine. The war is still going on and we're still shipping coal. Somebody's got to keep food and supplies in the store."

Wanda and Will came into the yard and stopped at a distance from Barlow.

Wanda pulled off her mask. "He's told you?"

Barlow sat with one elbow on the table, eyes and forehead partly covered by his hand. I knew that sign—his head ached.

"He's told me, but I'm not leaving. And I'm prepared to take care of Evie and Otis. We'll be as safe here as anywhere. Barlow? Are you all right?" He'd laid his head on the table.

"I'm fine, rather in need of sleep."

"And food," I said. "I'll fix your plate. Wanda, I'll bring plates for you too. Rest yourself at the table right there. I won't be a minute."

"The kids have to go," Will said. "Good Lord, if it was in my power, I'd send everyone who's well to a safe place. Charlie will bring a wagon tomorrow."

I'd never before been angry with Will, or seen him angry and insistent. Wanda's face was grim. Surely they were over-tired and in need of nourishment.

"I don't like it, but I agree with Will," Wanda said. "Tomorrow we'll be sending the kids to Granny's."

"All right, but if you feel different in the morning, have Charlie bring them here. Freddy and I will be staying. Sit now, I'll bring out your suppers."

She shook her head. "We've house calls to make. Barlow, talk some sense into her."

Barlow's smile was weary. "I'll talk, but I think we've heard her last word."

We kept our places a few moments, still and silent, until a cold breeze slid up from the ground, blowing leaves into Wanda's face. She brushed them away, sneezing. Then she said, "Stay well." She and Will left hand in hand.

Barlow kept his seat at the table. "Please," I said. "Come in. Move back to our room. I need you beside me."

"Soon. I'm sure I'll be with you soon."

"But not tonight."

"Not tonight."

CHAPTER 13

T he room was dark and Freddy was kicking the slats of the crib and crying, whimpers so loud I couldn't understand why they had not wakened Barlow.

More than anything, I wanted to start this day with Barlow beside me, rested and comforted by a night of sleeping close. Then we might sit in bed and drink coffee and speak of the day ahead while our limbs gathered strength and our eyes adjusted to the light of dawn.

I groped for Freddy and found him coiled in his blanket at the far end of his crib. He squirmed and fussed as I carried him into the kitchen, and when I sat down to nurse him, he turned his head away. His forehead seemed hot, and mine felt hot too.

I set him in the baby pen and put oats and water in a pot to stew, then washed and dressed, listening all the while to his whining. If only he could tell me the source of his unhappiness—painful gums or something else.

When I returned to the kitchen, Freddy's whimpers had turned to pitiful cries and he'd spit up, just a little on his nightgown, but frightening with so much sickness about. An ache began in the back of my neck and crawled to the top of my head.

I knocked on the bedroom wall to wake Barlow. When he answered, I said, "Freddy and I may be getting sick." I felt no panic, as though I'd been preparing for this discovery all along.

I heard his feet hit the floor. "I'm going for Will," he said.

Increasingly overcome with aches, I sat with Freddy in the rocking chair, trying to hold him close while he squirmed. Barlow entered the kitchen with Will and took Freddy from my arms. I'd ended our quarantine.

"Tell me how you feel," Will said.

"Afraid. Freddy is hot and fussy. He spit up."

"And you?"

"I don't know. Achy. Maybe."

"Now, Freddy, let me have these fingers," Will said, extracting Freddy's fist from his mouth. He felt the baby's forehead and ran a finger over his gums. "There's a few rough spots, teeth about to come through, but I don't think he's fevered." He tipped a small bottle of alcohol over a cloth and cleaned the end of a slender glass thermometer. "This has to be held in the mouth for five minutes, so I can't use it on a child." He shook the thermometer, put it under my tongue, and looked at his watch. I gripped the arms of the rocker and kept my eyes on my husband, who jiggled Freddy in his arms and smiled his worried assurance. If Freddy and I did not have the influenza, I'd just exposed us to the one person who'd been in greatest contact with it. If we did have it, we'd exposed Barlow.

"Okay, let's see this," Will said, taking the thermometer from my mouth. He held it up to the ceiling light and turned it in his fingers to see the reading. "Your temperature is elevated. One hundred and two degrees."

"But you think Freddy is fine?"

Will moved the end of his stethoscope over Freddy's chest and back. "I believe so.

A sudden sizzling turned our attention to the stove. Tears welled in my eyes. The oatmeal was boiling over.

CAROL ERVIN

"What should I do?"

Barlow set the oatmeal off the stove's hot eye. "Return to bed. I'll stay with Freddy."

I THREW UP IN A BUCKET BESIDE THE BED.

They kept the room dark. At times I heard their quiet steps and snatches of talk that seemed far away. Anytime I opened my eyes, Barlow or Wanda stood by my bed. Sometimes Will.

"Freddy," I said.

"He's fine."

This time it was Wanda.

"I hurt everywhere." My head felt like it was going to burst. I blinked and squeezed my eyes shut when a narrow glow at the door opened to a painful wall of light.

"May Rose." It was Barlow. He helped me sit and supported my back while Wanda put two pills in my mouth and held a water glass to my lips. "Drink," she said. One of the pills did not go down; it tasted terrible. "Again," she said. I had a hard time swallowing.

"Her pillow is wet," Barlow said.

He sat on the side of the bed and held me while Wanda changed the pillowcase. I thought of Freddy but had no desire to do anything but to lie down again.

Another time Barlow held me on his lap while Will placed the end of a stethoscope on my chest and back. "Her lungs don't sound too bad," Will said. "Does she cough much?"

"Too much. She never gets good rest."

They wanted me to sip some broth but I could not. Nothing mattered.

I wanted more blankets, but they said I was too hot. Wanda washed me in cool water, chattering away. "Ma, I was remem-

122

bering today how we told old Frank the Donnelly boys were trying to steal Hester's pigs."

"Shh," I said. "Luzanna."

"Luzanna would get a kick outa that story, but I'll never tell. I've never let on we knew her husband, or what a rotten kid he was."

"Shh, she's right over there."

"Ma, she's not."

"No?" I tried to raise my arm to point. "Right there in the corner."

"The fever's making you see things," she said.

"I'm cold. Cover me up."

I must have slept, though I never stopped being aware of the aches in my body and of voices that seemed to boom from the walls. My throat burned and my chest hurt from endless spells of coughing. They wiped sweat from my face and offered broth, but I could take no more than a swallow.

I woke one morning and slid my legs over the edge of the bed like it was an ordinary day. Then I lay back, too dizzy to do more. All was quiet, as though the whole town was shushed and listening. Barlow slept beside me.

He opened his eyes, sat up and felt my forehead. "Good morning. How do you feel?"

"All right. Thirsty."

"You don't feel as hot. Almost cool."

"I'd like to get out of bed and sit in a chair."

"I'll carry you."

I pushed away my covers. "I'd like to stand. Could you help me?"

"It's cold. I'll get your robe and house shoes."

He held my hand and helped me sit, lifted my legs over the edge of the bed and crouched to slide my house shoes onto my feet. Coming up, he gripped my arms, kissed my cheek and sighed. "I'm so glad you're better."

"I feel hollowed out."

He guided me to the easy chair in the kitchen and propped my feet on its hassock, then built up the fire in the stove and measured oatmeal into a pot.

I'd not seen the crib in our bedroom, and the baby pen was not in the kitchen. "Barlow!" I tried to stand but my legs were weak. "Where's Freddy?"

"He's at Luzanna's house. Glory and Virgie had him for a few days, then Luzanna took him. They say he's fine."

"You haven't seen him?"

"I've been here with you."

"When I was in bed, I was sure I heard him crying. Every day. How long have I been like this?"

"Ten days," Barlow said.

"Not the small flu."

"No, but you fought off the pneumonia. You need to be careful for a while."

I touched my flattened chest. "I guess my milk dried up."

"Wanda said it would likely be so."

"I'm so sorry." Weaning my child at eight months felt like a failure of duty. "When can Freddy come home?"

"I'll ask Will about that."

"But Freddy is well?" I glanced toward the place where the baby pen had been.

"I'm telling you true. Freddy is quite well. And you're getting better." He came to the chair and kissed my cheek. "I'm so thankful."

I needed to see my child.

Wanda came in the afternoon while Barlow went to his office.

She sat beside my bed and told the news. "We may be out of the woods, Ma. We've had no new cases of influenza and no deaths in the past three days."

"Freddy," I said.

"He's fine. He'll be spoiled rotten when he comes back—Luzanna's girls play with him all the time."

"I can't feed him anymore," I said.

"There's other ways. Luzanna knows what she's doing."

"When can he come home?"

"Soon as you feel like your old self. I want to fetch my kids from Granny's, too."

Talking wore me out. For the next two days I was in and out of bed. I took myself to the bathroom but needed Barlow to help me into a tub of warm water. Wanda washed my hair. On the third morning, I woke early, dressed without assistance, and cooked Barlow's breakfast. After that I had to lie down, but the next day I was stronger.

It was Sunday, and Barlow was home for the day, because like the school, church services had not resumed. "I feel good as new," I said. "Surely it's safe to bring Freddy home. Please, he's going to forget who I am."

Luzanna and Alma brought him that morning. He cried when he saw me, and I cried too. When they put him on my lap he seized my shirtwaist in his fists and nuzzled my chest. I cried again.

"It's all right," Luzanna said. "They have to be weaned sometime."

He squirmed in my arms. "He feels bigger, but maybe it's just me. I'm smaller." The bodice of my dress sagged to the waist.

"You'll fatten up," Luzanna said. "He's hungry. Let's show you what he can do."

I sat in one of the stuffed chairs with my feet on a hassock and watched Alma feed oatmeal to Freddy with a spoon. "He'll take water from a bottle, but not cow's milk," Luzanna said. "He likes the glass, and we get milk in him that way. To show me, she held a small glass to Freddy's lips. his lips chomped on the edge, and milk ran down his chin. "Will says he'll be fine; he's just having to grow up a bit faster."

"I know." I had a new sympathy for mothers whose only choice was to abandon their babies to the uncertain care of someone else. "Luzanna, I'm glad Freddy had you and your girls." In our case, the someone had not been a stranger, and our separation was over.

Late in the afternoon, Barlow returned the crib to our bedroom and the baby pen to the kitchen. When he set Freddy in the pen, Freddy gripped the bars and pulled himself up. "Look," Barlow said. "He's learned to stand."

Life had gone on without me. I wondered when I'd have the energy to catch up.

CHAPTER 14

"It's not right, me crowding your house," Luzanna said. She stood in my kitchen beside the new washing machine, running her customers' sheets through the wringer and letting them drop into a basket on the floor.

Wanda and Will had delivered the old washer to Etta Karakas, who had more dirty diapers than anyone else in town. With winter upon us, we'd moved the new machine inside. The atmosphere in the kitchen reminded me of washdays in the boardinghouse, with its steamy odors of wet cotton, bread rising, and beef boiling on the stove.

"Believe me when I say I'd rather have you here than not. I hate being alone. I was miserable when I lived up there on the mountain, and I wasn't much older than Alma. I had no family, no neighbors, and Jamie did not come home for weeks on end."

"I don't know how you took it."

"If I'd stayed any longer I'm sure I'd have lost my mind. But after Jamie ran off, I met Hester Townsend, and she let me work for room and board. Now I love having a houseful. People were always coming and going in the boardinghouse. I could live like that again."

Luzanna pushed aside the basket of wet sheets and set an empty one in its place. "I guess our bad days leave as strong a mark as the good. I remember plenty of times wishing I could have just one minute alone, like when I had my kids and Abner's too."

We seldom talked about our bad days. When we met, Luzanna had been traveling on foot with eight children, four belonging to Abner Hale, three of her own, and a baby they'd had together. The baby had died soon after, and Mr. Hale's youngest had died in my arms. We assumed Hale's surviving children were somewhere with his relatives.

"I can guess what days and nights are like for Etta Karakas," she said, "her with seven, and not one of them old enough for school."

The boiling beef was for Etta and her family. Luzanna and I were going to deliver it after school when Evie and Emmy arrived to babysit. The fact that Freddy had not suffered in someone else's care had taken away my reluctance to leave him with anyone other than his father. Like me, he seemed happiest when the house was full.

At the same time Emmy and Evie arrived from school, Blanche appeared with cookies from Piney. She stood inside the door and held the platter as we put on our coats. "These are for Etta. Piney said I couldn't go along 'less you said it was okay."

"We won't be staying," I said.

"But what if Etta wants us to stay?"

"People always say that. We should try to judge if they're just being polite or if they truly want us to be there."

"Like if you can see they need to be doing something instead of talking to us," Luzanna said.

Blanche turned down her pretty mouth. "If she needs to be doing something, it might be we could help."

Sometimes she seemed quite sensible.

At Etta's house, we quickly saw that though she might need to be doing something else, she was eager for us to stay and talk. She did not come to the door when Luzanna knocked, but called, "Come right in." We found her sitting on the front room floor, pulling a soggy diaper off one of the toddlers, who balanced himself by holding onto her shoulders and helped by raising one leg and then the other.

"This one don't like the potty," she said. Once unburdened by his wet pants, the boy tried to escape her clutches, but she held on and drew him back, swept him up, laid him on the floor and pinned on a diaper, fast as I'd ever seen it done. When she freed him, she dropped the diaper in a bucket and grimaced. "Sorry for the smell. And the mess. Try as I might, I can't keep this room no other way."

The room had gates at the entry to the kitchen and the stairway, and all seven children played there on the floor and on mattresses topped by tangled sheets. "They get on good together," she said. "Praise the Lord for that."

Blanche plopped down on a mattress and drew one of them onto her lap.

"That one's three and he's mine," Etta said, "though I can't hardly tell the difference no more. That boy I diapered is three, too, and he's got a twin. It was their ma that died. Marie and me was always expecting at the same time. We got two that are four and two that are five."

I clutched the pot of beef. "We're sorry for your loss. We don't want to interrupt your work. My husband said your Mother's Pension came through."

"That it did, and it makes me feel better about Milo working to feed all of us. He's a good man, and he's grieving plenty for these kids' ma."

Blanche uncovered the platter and passed out cookies.

"This is kind," Etta said. "It's way more than I deserve."

"Everyone deserves kindness," Luzanna said. "May Rose has a

beef boil in that pot. And I come along to see if there was anything I could do."

Etta lifted the gate to the kitchen. "Come in here and sit a while. I never get out, and almost nobody visits."

We sat in her kitchen and answered questions about ourselves. "My pa and his woman takes care of my babies," Blanche said.

Etta sighed. "That's wonderful."

"Well it is and it ain't. The little ones don't remember me. I run off, you see, and stayed away too long. I got lots of time to help you. Just let me know if you want to get out. I'll stay with your kids."

Once again Blanche surprised me with her grasp of the situation, but she also gave me a new worry. After we said our goodbyes and started home, I ran back for a last word with Etta. "I hope you will let Blanche visit again, but you should not leave her alone with the children."

"Oh, my, she wouldn't hurt them?"

"No, nothing like that. But she might forget what she's supposed to be doing. Leave them alone in the house. Something like that."

"I see," Etta said. "Well, I like her, so tell her to come back any time. You and Luzanna too."

I promised.

EARLY IN NOVEMBER, NEWSPAPERS BEGAN TO PREDICT THE END of the war. When it happened, word of the armistice spread from town to town before the news reached us in the paper. That Tuesday was sunny and warm for November, and when Barlow came home at noon, we set Freddy in his new stroller and went down to Main Street to celebrate with everyone else.

Open coal cars, full to brimming, waited on the rail sidings. "We've a contract for those," Barlow said. He did not need to say more to let me know what he was thinking. We were happy today, but tomorrow everything could change. Even the greenest miner must be aware that difficult times might lie ahead, but today work had been stopped for celebration, and they joked and jollied each other in the street. The war was over.

I felt happy, excited, and united with everyone as never before. Most of the sick had recovered, and no more of our young men would be drafted. That meant the young men closest to my heart—Charlie and Will—were safe. Barlow and I stopped in front of the store where Wanda stood, clutching Otis by the hand.

This spontaneous celebration was both a surge of hope and a release from the grief of the past, and I hadn't realized how much we needed it. School children waved small flags and paraded with their teachers in the street while their parents cheered from the sidewalk. When teachers directed the children back toward the school, men and women moved into the street, congratulating each other and passing jars of liquor. Mine guards passed through the crowd but appeared to take no notice of the jars.

"I need to go back to work. Come, I'll take you home," Barlow said.

I agreed that he should escort us, for the crowd was too tight and boisterous for comfort. A guard shoved past us toward a disturbance, prompting Wanda to climb the store steps for a better view. "It's a fight." Then she laughed. "What do you know, it's women."

Barlow turned the stroller to leave.

"Oh, my Lord," Wanda said. "It's Blanche."

"Barlow, wait while I see."

He touched my wrist. "You don't need to do anything; the guard's headed over there."

"She needs a friend." I hurried into the crowd. "Pardon me," I said again and again, working my way through knots of women standing on tiptoe and men sniggering into their jars. "Please, let me through." Still in a jolly mood, the onlookers obliged by making way.

I reached Blanche as the guards cleared a circle around her. She wasn't fighting; she lay on the ground with her arms raised to cover her head while a woman slapped it and pulled her hair. Another gave her a kick.

The guard seized the arm of the woman who was kicking. "That's enough. Go your way." Both women stepped back, but not too far, for the crowd had closed in around them. I stooped beside Blanche.

"Miss May Rose," she said. I helped her rise. She brushed street grit from her hands.

Meanwhile, the women babbled their defense to the guard.

"She's chasing my husband."

"And mine. Coming right up in his face like that, batting them eyes. Who does she think she is?"

One of the women worked her way past the guard and got nose to nose with Blanche. "Stay away, you little bitch, or you'll get worse than a shove."

I drew Blanche back, keeping my eyes on her alone. I didn't think the women would attack me, but I didn't want to do anything that might seem like a challenge.

"Go along, now," the guard said. "The show's over."

"I only said 'hello,'" Blanche said.

"Let's go." I put Blanche's arm through mine and walked her through the crowd.

Blanche looked over her shoulder. "They didn't really hurt me, but I don't know why they're mad."

"Let's talk about it later."

Barlow came toward us, beckoning to the mine guards to clear the street. The crowd was thinning.

Blanche grinned and squeezed my arm. "Are we going to your house?"

"For a little while." I held her hand, more for my comfort than hers. Barlow reached us and took my other hand in his.

"There's Wanda," Blanche said, when we got close to the store. "Is that your little baby? I haven't seen him for the longest time."

Wanda waited on the sidewalk, jiggling Freddy's stroller and hanging on to Otis. "Blanche," she scolded. "What was that fuss about?"

I shook my head. "Please, not now. Blanche and I will talk about it at home. Do you want to come with us?"

"I guess not," Wanda said.

Blanche bent over the stroller and wiggled Freddy's fingers. "Look how big."

"The street is clear now," Barlow said. "Can you manage the stroller alone?"

"I can help," Blanche said. She proceeded to push the stroller along the sidewalk. I waved to Barlow and hurried to catch up. At the road that turned uphill to our street, we met Charlie on his horse. He sat erect, like a soldier guarding the way. I wondered how much he'd seen.

Blanche let go of the stroller and waved. "Look there's Charlie. Charlie!"

I grabbed the stroller's handle. Charlie hesitated, then greeted us with a lift of his broad-brimmed hat.

"I'm going home with Miss May Rose," she said. "Do you want to come?"

He stared.

"Please?" Blanche tilted her head.

He squinted as though embarrassed, set his hat on his head and turned his horse away.

I sighed. When I wasn't worrying Charlie would be hurt in a fight, I worried some woman would drag him to the altar before he knew what was happening. I did not want that woman to be Blanche.

"I been wanting to see inside," Blanche said, when we reached my house.

I pulled out a kitchen chair and invited her to sit.

"Can I hold Freddy?"

"Let's put him in his high chair." I brought a piece of hard toast for him to chew. "I'm sorry about what happened today."

"It's all right."

"It's not all right, and you don't want it to happen again. Can you imagine why those women were angry with you?"

She shrugged. "They don't like me."

I wiped wet crumbs from Freddy's chin. "Remember what they said?"

"Husbands."

"Did you speak to their husbands?"

"Maybe."

"Did you smile at them?"

"They were smiling, too. It's not bad to smile."

"There are different ways to do it," I said. "With men, it's not good to look too long. If you smile and stare into their eyes, they'll get the wrong idea about you. Like their wives did today."

"They were riled, weren't they? I never get mad like some people."

"I know. You're a good person, Blanche, but I think you'll get into trouble if you're too friendly with other people's husbands."

"I don't like those men anyway," she said. "Nobody likes me here but you. Do you know how it feels when people don't like you?"

"I do."

"It makes me want to get away. Anywhere, I don't care. I just go. But Charlie is nice, and he's got no wife to bother me, does he? Maybe you could ask him to like me."

I didn't know how to answer. Fortunately, Blanche never seemed to mind a change of subject. "Would you like to see the house?"

"Oh, I would. Can I carry Freddy?" When I hesitated, she said, "I'm stronger than I look. I won't drop him."

I kept my eyes on her as she carried Freddy through every room. "Your pa built a lot of this," I said.

"He works all the time, and Piney took my kids somewhere and I don't know what to do."

"Piney says sometimes you forget about the children. When they're little, you have to take care of them all the time until they're big enough to take care of themselves. Remember Etta Karakas? She said you could come back anytime. She needs help with all those children."

"That's right, she did. I think I'm not good at remembering. Will you ask Charlie to be my friend?"

It seemed she was not going to forget about Charlie. "I'm not sure he wants friends. But if I get a chance, I'll ask."

✿

THE END OF THE WAR SPIKED A FEVER OF NEW CONCERNS FOR miners and coal operators alike. I knew Barlow was worried because he stopped telling me about his work day. Instead, he became even more attentive to Freddy and me, as though he needed a diversion. I responded by cooking his favorite foods, giving my hair an extra brushing before he returned from work, sharing only good news, and waking him with a kiss each morning.

The loaded coal trucks had not moved from their railroad sidings since the announcement of the armistice in Europe. For now, it almost didn't matter that the price of coal had fallen, because manufacturers and shippers weren't buying—they already had huge stockpiles.

When he let slip the topic of a meeting with Will and Randolph, I suggested they come to dinner at our house and let Wanda and me listen to their discussion. I had to persuade him. "Difficult business goes down better with good food, don't you think? Besides, I'd rather know your problems than not. Wanda and I won't say anything unless you ask us, and you won't have to go over all of it later for my benefit."

The topic was as hard to take as bad medicine, but if my husband had to endure it, I wanted to know everything. They were going to talk about mine layoffs.

That afternoon as I prepared dinner, Blanche appeared at my door, shivering in the cold wind.

"Pa's gone to fetch Piney home before the snow comes," she said.

I invited her into the kitchen. "Did you forget your coat?"

"I put it in the box at the church," she said. "For the refugees."

"Oh, Blanche. You don't have another?"

"Not at present."

"You weren't supposed to give your only coat."

She warmed her hands by the cook stove. "I didn't need it then," she said.

It seemed best to let her stay and help. Together we moved the parlor chairs and baby pen from the kitchen so there would be room for five chairs at the dining table. "It's a business meeting," I said, when she asked who was coming. "After dinner, the men will be discussing mine business."

"I guess I wouldn't like it," she said.

"Not this time."

"Your house is cold everywhere but the kitchen," she said, when we carried a chair to the front room. "But you got a nice lookout. You can see the whole town and look down on everybody. That's what folks say—you set yourself apart and look down on everybody." Blanche smiled as though she were stating a compliment, but her words surprised me, and they stung.

"They say that?"

"I'd be lonely up here," she said. "Nobody behind or beside you. And your house ain't half finished."

"Someday everything will be different." Wounded and sad, I hurried her back to the warm kitchen.

"Is Charlie coming to dinner?"

"No, he has nothing to do with the mine."

"Mr. Randolph will be here, I bet. And Miss Glory? He's got an eye for her; I see him watching her in church."

"Glory will not be here. Why don't you go home now and cook something nice for when your pa and Piney come home?"

"Pa said he'd bring them by suppertime. Can I come tomorrow?"

"Tomorrow is Saturday, and we'll be going to Virgie's in the afternoon. I don't know if Piney will come or not, but when you see her, ask what you can do to help." I gave her a shawl and sent her on her way with a pumpkin pie.

☙❧

I WAS SORRY I COULD NOT INCLUDE GLORY IN OUR DINNER party, for had she been present, Randolph Bell might not have eaten his dinner with such a grim expression. But it was impossible to ask her without including Virgie, and Virgie's presence at the table might make the men reluctant to discuss business. I was also afraid that Glory would not appreciate being cast as Randolph's dinner partner.

The men's work began after Wanda and I cleared away the dishes and brought coffee to the table.

"I hate to see anyone laid off," Will said. "Their families have barely recovered from the epidemic. To lose your child or your wife, and now your work?"

To lose your husband, the breadwinner of your family, I thought. The widows and children of four miners who'd died in the epidemic had already left town. It was impossible to help all sad conditions or even keep them in mind for very long, but I worried how the combined family would survive if Milo Karakas had no work.

Cooking had left the room hot, and when I noticed Randolph putting a finger in his collar to loosen it from his neck, I opened the door an inch, admitting a draft to cool us.

Randolph looked pointedly at Will, then Barlow. "We've an opportunity now to dismiss the least productive workers." He didn't say "fire," a distasteful word to all, but the nicer word did not soften the meaning. "If the workers had a union, they'd be telling us what to do. We'd have to keep men with seniority, even if they were incompetent or dangerous to themselves and everyone else."

"That's the only good thing about our present situation," Will said. "We can still make the decisions. What do you think about cutting everyone back to two or three days?"

"If we cut everyone to less than three days, the best of them will leave," Randolph said. "This may be our last chance to dismiss the ones who aren't good at their jobs. I think we should do it now. Barlow, what can we afford?"

Barlow passed a sheet of ledger paper to each of his partners, printed in his small, precise numerals. "We have about two months of income for coal already sold, but as you see, plenty of outstanding debt, plus payroll. And we've had no new orders since the armistice."

The men studied Barlow's figures. I supposed it was easier to make decisions while looking at numbers on paper and not at the faces of workers and their families.

Barlow passed a second sheet to Will and Randolph. "This shows projected payroll for the next two months with one shift, giving all the men two days. But we'll have to stockpile our own coal and hope demand recovers. I've left out payments to ourselves."

Randolph squinted at the figures. "You mean our salaries will be in addition to what's here?

"No," Will said. "He means we'll take nothing during that time. I assume we all have something saved?"

Barlow never spoke of our finances, so I had no idea if we were rich or moderately secure. If he was suggesting the partners go two months without reimbursement, he must be certain we would not suffer. I thought Will and Randolph might be better off, for they had not built and furnished a large house.

"I'll get by," Randolph said. "And a slowdown will be better than closing the mine."

"Some mines in the association have already shut down, and I know there are closures throughout the country," Barlow said. "We'll be helped by decreased production everywhere, plus the fact that it's winter and stockpiles of coal for home heating were kept low during the war. Eventually manufacturers will sell their surplus goods, but for now they're laying off workers too. We have to look ahead: newspapers are forecasting a boom in electrification in rural areas, so it will be smart to develop connections with new electric power plants. We'll go through some adjustments, but things will get better. Until then, I think our country is in for a hard time."

Hard times were hardest on the poor. I lowered my eyes to avoid showing my reaction and tried to listen instead of thinking of all that could go wrong.

"I've had hard times most of my life, but never when I had employees to consider," Will said. "Or a family."

For a few moments there was no response but a rattling of papers. Then my husband spoke. "Towns destroyed in the war are going to be rebuilt. We'll be shipping coal again, though I can't say when. For sure, we can't pay the men to produce if we can't sell the product. They have to see that. But here's what concerns me most: operators of union mines have been encouraging the United Mine Workers to get down here and organize our men. They want to level the playing field for themselves, you see, by making our coal as expensive to produce as theirs."

"We can't blame them for that," Will said. "So you think our men will strike for union representation?"

"If we don't give them that right, they'll strike, no matter what other concessions we make."

"Then let's work them in full force until that time," Randolph said. "When they strike, we'll have our own stockpiles."

"You two know more about this than I do," Will said. "But what if the UMW doesn't come? We'll have coal we can't sell, and men we can't pay. Then we'll have to shut down."

"Make no mistake, the UMW is on its way." Barlow sounded grim. "The association will reject their demands and the men will stop work. So what do you think, shall we work the men two or three days, or go full-force for a shorter time?"

"With the other mines laying off, the men may appreciate us keeping them on," Randolph said.

Like me, Wanda had been sitting quietly. Now she spoke. "Even so, when the time comes, they'll strike."

I lifted my head and saw the men nod, one after the other. We seemed to be at the brink of our own war. Thoughts of Etta and her family ended my pledge of silence. "Will they be able to get food at the store? Stay in their houses?"

"Ladies," Randolph said, "we'll do what we can to prevent anything happening here like at Paint Creek. If the men strike for union representation, we'll be less able to control our future. We'll be caught between the strikers and whatever the association votes to do. Our miners won't be able to choose independently, either—they'll be compelled to act in accord with all the other miners in the region. The union will try to get them to hold out and not break the strike."

"A lot of organizing will have to take place before then," Will said. "And I don't think they'll strike in the dead of winter. So maybe we'll have time to prepare. Wanda and I have treated the sick in nearly every house in Winkler, and I believe our employees will want to treat us fairly. I hope they'll resist the union, especially if we can somehow let them know the Winkler Mine will be casting a vote for a higher wage."

Randolph returned his set of papers to Barlow. "Will we do that? Vote for a higher wage?"

"We can do it, but our vote won't count for much against the rest of the association," Barlow said.

A chilling wind blew open the door, and Randolph rose and closed it. "If they strike, will we let them run up debt at the store? What will we do if we get new orders? Hire scabs?"

Barlow shrugged. "Most of the association will hire temporary workers. If we want to stay in business we won't have a choice, no more than the men will be able to go against their brothers. We'll have to go along with the other operators."

It was a dirty word, scabs, the miners' term for men who crossed their picket lines and took their jobs. In other mine towns, labor agents had brought them in by the trainload, men in need of a job who had no idea they were being taken into hostile territory. Surely it didn't have to be this way. If operators respected their workers and the dangers they faced, paid a decent wage, treated them fairly and kept in mind their families' needs, there would be no need for such a bitter division between them. But time and again Barlow reminded me that the biggest mines were owned by distant shareholders who had no human connection with their employees.

"What a pickle," Wanda said.

"If the men strike, we could let their families stay in the houses a week or two, and tell them the store will have no more provisions at the end of that week," Will said. "I suppose we'll need more guards. And the store should stop selling guns and ammunition now."

Guns and ammunition. I glanced at the others. Everyone looked grim.

"They'll strike," Barlow said. "If we want to fill new orders

CAROL ERVIN

during the strike, we'll have to hire replacements. Those workers will need our company houses."

With that gloomy pronouncement, the meeting came to an end. That night I woke frequently, unable to escape thoughts of Etta Karakas and seven small children living through the winter in a tent.

CHAPTER 15

Saturday afternoon I met Piney on her corner and we walked together to Virgie's house. I'd been looking forward to an afternoon of silly talk to lift my mind from dismal thoughts, and seeing Piney was a great start.

"I'm glad to see you looking good, with what we heard of your bad time," she said. "We brought Ma with us for the winter, did you know? We just about had to hog-tie her to the wagon. Why do folks insist on things that's against the best?"

"It's a deep question. Some people are always sure they know best, and some like me are never certain what the best is."

"That's the truth of it. Ma is one who never doubts herself. I need to thank you—Simpson says you been a friend to Blanche. You don't know how we appreciate that. I left the kids with her today. At least she thinks I did. Simpson's gonna keep an eye on them."

"Blanche is a sweet girl," I said.

"That she is, though she's not got a lick of common sense. But guess what, she and Ma are getting along real fine. She says 'Yes, Ma'am and 'No, Ma'am, and rushes to do whatever Ma says."

"She likes taking orders?"

"She does indeed. And you know Ma is the bossiest of bosses."

"Will wonders never cease? We've missed you, Piney."

At Virgie's, we learned that Wanda would not be attending the gathering that day. "She and Evie are having a piano lesson," Glory said. "And they're in the process of moving their furnishings out of the store, since there are empty houses now."

True to his word, Randolph had given notice to half a dozen miners, presenting them with lists of infractions that in a time of slow business he could no longer ignore. Will and Wanda visited the houses of workers who'd been fired, carrying a basket of food and good wishes for a successful life in another place. Then the mine guards, whose numbers had doubled, stood by to make sure the families made a peaceful exit from town. I watched them go from my front window, feeling responsible for their fate. Barlow said Randolph had tried to impress on the men that they might do much better in a different line of work. Even if the workers respected his word, I doubted they could believe this loss was in their best interests.

There had to be anxiety in every home, because since the armistice, the men never knew if the mine had work for the day until they heard the shift whistles. This week our miners had worked four days and next week it might be three. Our loaded coal cars remained on railroad sidings with dozens of cars from other mines, and we were accumulating mountains of coal around the tipple. Soon the workers would have lots of free time to talk about organizing. When Barlow was home he spent more time playing baby games with Freddy, and he kissed me at odd times, as though delighted about something. He didn't fool me, but I was glad he'd turned to play instead of being mean and short tempered.

At Virgie's, everyone made a fuss about having Piney with us again. This afternoon Luzanna, Piney and I were to knit small mittens while Glory and Virgie cut patterns from newspaper for children's coats. At some future time we intended to assemble them from garments donated to war refugees and never shipped. None of us said anything about the Winkler Mine dismissals, but our talk was full of unease about other changes in town, like workmen loitering on the street.

I shared my one piece of good news. "Barlow plans to hire a few miners skilled in carpentry to work on our house the days they're off."

The others agreed this was wonderful, but my mention of layoffs led to a flurry of talk, including the possibility of a strike. Such speculation made us solemn, and for a while we attended to our work with no sound but the click of knitting needles and the crackle of Virgie's paper patterns. Then Glory said, "During all that sickness, I felt like everyone was united. So many were like Will and Wanda, helping each other, taking care of the sick in the church. We cried together over every death. A strike will pull us apart."

Virgie folded a set of pattern pieces, wrote a size on the top one and fastened them with a pin. "That's enough gloom for today. We've better news. Guess who's getting married? Grady Malone!"

Sounds of satisfaction passed around the room. I'd stopped worrying about Grady, but was glad to hear he was settling down. "This should put an end to talk about him and Wanda."

Virgie hooted. "This hitching won't put an end to talk. He's marrying a schoolgirl. The bride and her mother came here and bought one of our dresses. We had to let it out at the waist because she's in the family way, poor thing. Just a schoolgirl."

Like shameless gossips, we wanted to know the girl's name. It shouldn't have been so, but I think we were relieved to learn she was no one we knew.

"I suppose Alma knows her," Luzanna said. "I wouldn't use a shotgun to force the wretch to the altar; I'd direct it to his private parts. No, of course I couldn't do that. But maybe again I would, if it was my girl and I happened to have a shotgun in my hands."

145

Luzanna's earnest confusion gave us a smile.

"I fear her parents are forcing this marriage," Glory said. "She seemed so gloomy, I wonder if she likes him at all."

Our glee dissolved. To lift the mood, we told Piney about the welfare committee and our new project of sewing clothes for children. She had another concern. "Ruby tells me some of the kids bring nothing to school for lunch. If things get worse, do you suppose we could take something there for them to eat?"

"I'm sure we can't feed them all," Virgie said.

"People has to do what they can," Piney said. "The corn harvest was good, and Simpson has plenty of cornmeal at the mill."

"We should stock up on staples," I said, "not just for ourselves, but to help feed the children. You know, in the event that worse comes to worst. We won't be able to watch them starve, will we?"

When I reached home that afternoon I had a suggestion for Barlow. "As long as the men are on reduced wages, why not stop charging for their house coal? You wouldn't have to say a thing about it, just forget to subtract the coal charge from their pay. They might not notice what you'd done, and even if they did, I doubt they'd say anything."

For the first time since the slowdown in orders, a genuine smile brightened his dark eyes. "Will and Randolph will like this. And the association need never know."

I think he was as pleased at fooling the association as he was happy to do something for the workers.

AS OTHER MINES IN THE REGION SLOWED PRODUCTION, MEN came to Winkler looking for work, among them carpenters. With a new sense of opportunity, Barlow's voice turned bright and brisk. "May Rose, this is our chance to finish the house." When I didn't immediately respond, he mellowed. "You don't approve?"

"I only wonder if this is a good time." Some wives might have hesitated to question their husbands, but mine had lived many years with his sister, whose good sense had taught him that a challenge or contradiction from a woman was in no way a threat to a man's position as head of the house.

"We have to go forward in faith," he said. "It's the only way."

Keeping things as they were seemed safer, but I thought he was right on one thing: without confidence in our steps, we would most certainly fall backwards.

Now on some days there were as many as six workmen in our house. With men hammering, dropping lumber, shouting at each other and tracking through the kitchen to the basement, living there became difficult. So one Saturday, the workmen moved our furniture into a company house on Main Street. The move down in quality was an improvement in terms of space, for there I had a front room for sitting, two upstairs bedrooms, and a kitchen dedicated to cooking and consuming meals. Though being on Main Street meant more noise and dirt, I looked forward to the prospect of having neighbors.

In our other house, everyone came and went through the kitchen door, not the front, so I was surprised, the day after we moved in, by a knock at the front. With Freddy on my hip, I opened the door to find Miss Graves on the step with two older women, all holding onto their hats in the cold wind.

I invited them to hurry inside. Miss Graves introduced them as my nearest neighbors, her landlady, Mrs. Greggorio, and Mrs. Cox. I'd seen Mrs. Cox in church—she was the president of the Ladies' Aid.

Mrs. Greggorio was stout with thick black eyebrows, black hair and a hint of dark hair on her upper lip. Mrs. Cox seemed her opposite, having thin arms, small gray eyes, no eyebrows, and a turned-down mouth. Each held out a welcome gift, a fruitcake and a bowl of stewed pumpkin, and they looked as uncomfortable as I felt. I tried to greet them as I might welcome a well-loved friend, inviting them to sit, nervously certain that Miss Graves must have shamed them into coming. She held Freddy while I set their gifts in the kitchen. Then I hurried to pass a platter of Piney's sugar cookies.

In spite of her small size, Mrs. Cox spoke in deep, husky tones, and I was surprised when her turned-down mouth turned up. "I live with my son, Horace. He's working on your house," she said. "So I want to say we're glad of the extra work."

I'd wondered what we'd find to talk about, and this announcement was a surprising start. I'd have to ask Barlow to point out Mrs. Cox's son, because I'd tried to stay out of the way of the workmen and hadn't bothered to learn their names. I was beginning to think such avoidance might be a fault. I returned her smile. "My husband and I are very grateful for his help."

"We want to thank you for what you did when all was so sick," Mrs. Greggorio said.

I sat on the loveseat beside Miss Graves and Freddy. "My part was very small, but I hope it helped someone. Did your families have sickness?" I was afraid to ask if any of them had died. Mrs. Cox wore widow's black.

Mrs. Greggorio helped herself to a second cookie. "My girls and their kids was sick, but they didn't have it too bad, and their men kept working. We heard you got it yourself. Folks was praying for you."

I was overcome by the idea of prayers on my behalf, and surprised that anyone beyond my circle had known I was sick.

"Your washing machine was a godsend," Mrs. Cox said. "Without it women would never of kept up with the dirty bedding and the like."

Mrs. Greggorio nodded. "Times is always hard for common folks, though I'd say me and Mrs. Cox are not so bad off as some of the young ones who've got big families. Lots of us are praying the men won't vote to strike. You must hear the talk—it's all over."

I acknowledged I'd heard it. I'd wanted to have friends among the miners' wives, but now I was afraid to hear what they would say next, perhaps a question I should not answer or a request I could not fulfill.

"We thought you should know there's no real hard feelings against the Winkler Mine or you and the doctor's wife," Mrs. Cox said. "Whatever comes."

"The men have been patient about their wages all through the war," I said. "I'm sure my husband will vote to give them a raise, though you must know the mine is not currently selling coal. I don't know if he will be able to convince other operators. I often wish we were not tied to decisions of the coal association."

"So far the Winkler Mine has been more than fair," Mrs. Cox said, "but you've heard of Paint Creek?"

I nodded, afraid that anything I said might be taken the wrong way.

"The men will do what they must do," Mrs. Greggorio said. "Meanwhile, us women should try to stay on good terms. Right now we're all concerned about these new guards."

"The guards? Are they abusing anyone?"

"Not that we've heard," Mrs. Cox said. "But the men have enough to worry them. They don't need guards lined up on both sides of the portal, watching them come and go. It makes a bad feeling, don't you know. One wrong word either way and there could be fights, for some of our men is hotheads. I figure some of the guards is hotheads too."

I promised to learn what I could about the new guards. "I'm sure we don't want any unnecessary harassment. Or hatred."

Miss Graves bounced Freddy on her knees and smiled at his giggles. "Hatred is as bad as fire in a coal seam. Once it catches hold, nobody can put it out or stop it from spreading. I try to teach that in school."

"Whatever comes, I hope we women can stick together," I said.

My neighbors agreed. "But when somebody on your side is hurt by a body on the other, it makes you hate them, don't you see," Mrs. Greggorio said. "It's like a feud. The feelings strike deep and stay put."

"I think we understand each other," Mrs. Cox said. "The Bible teaches we should love our enemies. I don't mean to say we're enemies, but maybe you can imagine how things will get if there's a strike."

We parted with vows to remember each other in our prayers, no matter what.

CHAPTER 16

As Barlow had predicted, the need for heating in December stimulated new orders. It was a relief to hear the slam of coal cars coupling on the rails and to know our miners were making do on three days of work a week. I supposed they were making do, for none of them left.

"I'm afraid I have disturbing news," Barlow said, the morning after an association meeting. The sky was not yet light, and we were talking quietly over our first cup of coffee. I'd been awake when he'd returned late in the night, but he'd been agitated and too tired to talk.

"It's not that we haven't been expecting it," I said.

He reached for my hand. "This is nothing we expected. It's about Milo Karakas. Etta's brother-in-law."

"Milo! Was there an accident? Is he badly hurt?" In spite of their misfortunes, Etta maintained a brave outlook. I'd convinced myself that she and her brother-in-law were managing as well as any.

"Milo's name is on a list of union organizers. The association wants them all to be fired and blacklisted."

I pulled my hand away. "Barlow, you can't fire him. He provides for seven small children!"

"We've ignored the association's blacklist before, but with all the talk of strikes, this time it's more serious. We'll have to see what we can do. You can be sure we don't like taking orders from the association. Only a few other operators think like we do, that we must give our men the right to organize. Otherwise..."

"Otherwise, Paint Creek."

"I hope it won't be that bad. There was a lot to learn from Paint Creek. I told the association we must do better by our employees. Randolph and I tried to impress the fact that we're less than a day's travel from union mines, too close to ignore them any longer. Unfortunately, many of the absentee owners believe that men who dig coal are not fully human, otherwise they would not risk their lives blasting underground, would not come out of the mine black with coal dust, would not live so poorly, drink so much and be so foolish as to deprive their families of food and shelter by going out on strike."

I hated everything about the coal business, the dirt and dangers, the politics and hatreds it stirred, yet families needed heat and men needed work. And I feared Barlow had invested almost all his resources in the Winkler Mine.

"Three mines in the association have closed down," he said. "Permanently, I understand."

"But Milo Karakas, Barlow. What will you do?"

"We won't fire him, not immediately, but we'll tell him about the blacklist, and let him know the association may force our hand. It's a shame, Randolph says he's a bright young man, the kind to make superintendent. But he's also a strong supporter of his fellow workers, and these men stick together like family."

I thought there was something to admire in that.

A day later, Barlow reported they would not have to fire Milo Karakas after all. "He's been hired by the United Mine Workers.

It gets us out of a spot, but Randolph is sorry to lose him. They get along well, and Milo knows Randolph had plans for him."

"It may help to have someone you trust on the other side," I said. "Someone who won't be hostile toward us from the start. And if all goes well, he might want to work for you again. Will he be able to stay in his house?"

"No, of course that's not possible. Don't worry, the union will help him find a place. But you know, he'll be working for miners and dealing with operators throughout the region. Those experiences may erode any feelings of loyalty he has toward us."

It was Blanche who brought the news of the Karakas family's relocation. "They've got a place outa town, and they're gonna have a milk cow," she said. "But I'm gonna miss Etta so bad. She says it won't be far to walk to see her when the weather's not bad. Or maybe Charlie can take me on his horse."

"Charlie?"

"You know who I mean. Your Charlie. He gave me a ride, just the other day. I said we could both sit on the horse but he walked and let me ride. Ain't he sweet?"

I didn't know what to say.

"Etta has to move to the other house real quick, for it won't be long before we have snow," Blanche said. "I'm gonna ride with her and the kids in the wagon, and Charlie will fetch me home."

I HAD QUESTIONS FOR WANDA WHEN SHE BROUGHT OTIS THE next morning, but she stalled them with a request. "Will wants you to convince Barlow the mine should pay for milk for the school kids." She pulled off Otis's knitted cap and unbuttoned his coat.

"Convince Barlow?" It wasn't hard to see what was behind this. Barlow must already have refused. "He's worrying now about every penny."

She set Otis at my table and put Freddy's wooden truck in front of him. "Four milk cans, twice a week. Will says if the miners' kids drink anything but water, it's coffee. He says milk would make a difference in their growth and health. It's plain to see if you compare Otis to other boys his age. Simpson's grandkids get milk, too. And what's that you're feeding Freddy?"

It was small bites of toast softened in warm milk. "I'm sure Barlow wants to help the children, but it's not fair to ask me to change his mind."

"You got him to give them coal."

"Another loss of income. I'd like all the children to have milk, but at present I think my husband needs me to support his decisions."

"So no milk?"

"I won't try to convince him. I suppose you might try. Or Glory."

"Glory! I'll bet she could do it. Glory's not afraid of her Uncle Barlow."

"It's unfair to say I'm afraid of Barlow. Your husband doesn't have to worry about coal sales and mine expenses, but these things are Barlow's responsibility. He tries not to show it, but I know they keep his head in an uproar. At home I'd like him to have some peace."

"That's all right; we don't need you—we have Glory."

"Fine," I said. "But if she asks him, please have her do it in his office, not here."

"Good enough." Wanda kissed Otis. "Be a good boy and play nice with Freddy."

"Don't go yet. I have a question for you. Charlie and Blanche —is something going on?"

"I see them walking together about every day," Wanda said.

"Oh, my. I thought Blanche might be content with Etta for a friend and your granny to boss her around."

"That don't mean she's stopped wanting Charlie. I've changed my mind. It might not be so bad, them being together, if Uncle Russell can stand it. Think on the good side—Charlie is finally making up with somebody new."

"I didn't say it was bad. See if you can talk with him, just to find out if Blanche is a bother or if he likes her hanging around."

"Okay. Glory will talk with Barlow and I'll talk with Charlie. And here's some news that pleases me no end. Because of Grady's shotgun wedding, the school board fired him. From now on I'm gonna lead the singing at church!"

◈

IN THOSE TENSE WEEKS, MOST MEN STOPPED ATTENDING church. Wanda said they used Sunday mornings to meet with workers in other towns. Either from respect or fear, the preacher made no notice of their absence, and said nothing from the pulpit about workers or owners.

We looked ahead with apprehension and worked with new fervor. Two Sundays before Christmas, Miss Graves assigned readings and announced after-school rehearsals for a children's play to be performed Christmas Eve. Glory also stood in front of the congregation and announced a holiday workshop for mothers five evenings a week in the school. "There will be sewing machines, patterns, and donated material," she said. Because the children were present, she did not explain the purpose, but the women immediately understood that the workshop would be dedicated to Christmas gifts.

Glory and Virgie's workshop contributed hope and satisfaction to a season threatened by layoffs, a strike, and maybe worse. I worked those evenings with Miss Graves, who organized older girls to conduct games for the children while their mothers were busy sewing in another room. She also used some of that time to rehearse the children's parts for the play. Meanwhile, their mothers were sewing and stuffing cloth animals and dolls. The school rooms burst with progress, and each night I walked home with new certainty that everything would come out right.

A week before Christmas, miners throughout our region rejected the new contract on several grounds, one being that it did not allow them to form a union. The next day no one reported for work.

I worried there would be violence. "Barlow, please do what you can to restrain everyone," I said. "Tell the guards not to provoke the men."

"Randolph has spoken to the men and guards about the battles that can erupt during a strike," he said. "We'll order our guards to disregard bad language and try not to overreact to a bit of stone-throwing. If the men set up a picket line at the portal, Will, Randolph and I will be there. Most respect Randolph and have good reason to be grateful to Will. We'll try to go wherever men congregate to let them know we're working for a good and peaceful resolution."

"And they won't be turned out of their houses, or refused credit at the store?"

"We shouldn't talk of that now," he said.

It wasn't the answer I needed to hear.

That day I bundled Freddy in blankets and visited my neighbors, first Mrs. Greggorio and then Mrs. Cox. "My friends and family are in sympathy with the miners," I said. "We want things to turn out well for all of us."

We agreed that in the matter of our husbands' jobs we had no power and could make no promises. "We must put action into what we believe most," Mrs. Cox said. "Peace on earth, good will toward men."

We clasped each other's hands, wanting those words to come true. I didn't know if Mrs. Cox had any particular action in mind, but I hoped it meant the women she knew would encourage their husbands to behave in a peaceful manner. I could only hope they'd prevail.

CHAPTER 17

C hristmas workshops at the school continued, though laughter among the miners' wives was replaced by an undercurrent of secretive talk. The children also seemed on edge, with episodes of misbehavior, a first-grader who cursed, several who wet their pants, and a toddler who caused an uproar by biting the hands of other children. Miss Graves and I shared our anxious wish for a peaceful Christmas Eve.

Each morning that week our workers manned a picket line at the portal, but it was relaxed, because the strike was in its early days and no replacements had appeared anywhere in the region. The wives were polite when I was near. My heart ached.

"The association is hiring agents to bring in replacements," Barlow said. "I was asked how many we wanted."

"And you replied?"

"I said none for the time being. Randolph says these agents go to the cities and round up anyone unemployed, including derelicts, drunkards, and men with no experience in any kind of mining or machine work. Sometimes they get immigrants right off the boat, men who can't speak a word of English. All these poor souls are fooled by promises of good homes and wages and seldom understand they may face opposition from the men whose jobs they'll be taking. The operators hope the sight of men crossing the picket lines will make the strikers give in, and they won't actually have to use those wretched replacements."

He and Randolph had addressed our miners from the store steps. "We told the men we don't want to bring in replacements. We said we hoped they'd understand that while the store would remain open, we could give no more credit."

"Lord," I said. "What will they do?" After paying their store bills from the previous week, most employees had little left, and some never made enough to catch up.

"I'm told some women and children may go to families elsewhere, if they have them."

"Did the men ask if we were going to turn them out of their houses?"

"They did. We said we don't want to evict them, but everything depends on the length of the strike. We have our creditors to pay. It won't last forever, May Rose. Eventually the mine will have to start up again, either with our current employees or with new hires."

Two nights before Christmas Eve, my friends and I carried bread and butter sandwiches to the school. Miss Graves attempted to keep the children from shoving and grabbing as we passed the sandwiches, but finally we had to lift the trays over our heads and shout at them to sit down. At Will's direction, Russell and Charlie brought in four metal cans of milk. The children were not accustomed to drinking milk, but they were hungry enough to try anything. That night I walked home with Glory and Virgie, all of us sadder than before.

Glory was fervent about our cause. "We need to feed the children as long as we have flour to bake bread."

I agreed, but Virgie said, "All our notions may change if the strike goes on and on."

SINCE CHARLIE HAD ADVANCED IN SOCIABILITY TO THE POINT of allowing Blanche into his small circle, I decided it was time he came under a roof other than his own.

"Charlie," I said. "I want you and Russell to come to our house for Christmas dinner." I'd also invited Luzanna and her children. Glory and Virgie were entertaining Will and Wanda, Evie and Otis.

Charlie mumbled.

"I'm sorry, will you say that again, please?"

"Her," he said. "Blanche."

"You want me to invite Blanche also?"

"Her house."

"You're going to her house Christmas day?"

He nodded. I wondered if anyone had told Piney.

Piney stopped to see me that day on her way to the store. She always cheered me, being pleasant by nature and never having anything to say about mining or the strike. "Yes, Blanche invited him, so I asked Russell, too," she said. "I hope that's all right. You could all come if we had more room." Her plump face was full of smiles. "The children are so excited about Christmas. It's going to be a lovely time, Blanche and Ma getting along so good, and now Charlie coming to the house, can you believe that? He's a sweet young man. I hope Ma won't be jealous—she acts like Blanche is hers alone."

I was a little jealous that Charlie's first visit to a house other than his own would not be mine. I promised we'd call to exchange Christmas greetings later in the day.

Mild weather on Christmas Eve resulted in the church over-flowing, not just with the regular congregation, but with farm families from the nearby hills and valleys. I was surprised to see one of my former students, Ebert Watson's son Jonah, sitting near the front with our Miss Graves. I hadn't heard of Jonah for a long time, not even a mention of his name by Miss Graves. If he was her choice, she'd made a good one. When they were all students in my little schoolroom, both Evie and Alma had been sweet on him.

The evening seemed an occasion for other young men and women to sit together. I gave particular attention to the boy beside Alma, one I had not seen before, who unlike others his age wore a suit and tie.

"That's Alma's new boyfriend," Evie said. "His pa is the super-intendent at the Barbara. Every girl in school is jealous." She grinned. "Me, too."

"You're too young to be thinking about boys," I said. Of course she wasn't. I only wished.

Peace reigned through the evening, enhanced by pride in the children's songs and recitations even when they could not be distinctly heard, by laugher for a play full of slapstick humor, and by the simple wooden toys passed out at the end by Simpson dressed as Santa Claus. Barlow distributed sacks of oranges and peppermint candy, and at the end of the evening, Randolph read the name of each Winkler Mine employee, and each came forward to receive a ham.

"We've reached the limit of what we can do," Barlow said, when we talked about everything the next morning. "Soon we'll have to produce coal again, with or without these men."

THE DAY AFTER CHRISTMAS, THE OPERATOR OF A MINE OWNED by the railroad called on Barlow at home. Barlow introduced the man as Hollis Stone. He was half a foot taller than Barlow and looked quite stout, bundled in a heavy overcoat, scarf, and Bowler hat. With his broad white moustache, he resembled our former President, William Howard Taft.

Stone removed his hat and peeled tight gloves from his hands.

"I thought talking here might be preferable to your office. There's quite a crowd of men assembled outside."

Barlow laid Stone's coat over the stair railing and motioned him to sit. "This is fine, as long as you'll allow my wife to be present. I am regularly improved by her opinion."

"Of course, of course. Pleased to include you, Mrs. Townsend." Neither his face nor his tone conveyed pleasure.

Though the interior walls of the company house were planked instead of plastered, I thought our front room looked quite nice. For the first time in almost two years, we were using the parlor furnishings we'd bought for the new house. Mr. Stone, however, looked around with the air of one confused. "I suppose this is tolerable for a short time," he said. "Residing here, I mean. You've something better under construction?"

"That's correct," Barlow said. I clenched my hands, certain my husband shared my irritation, and impressed by how well his manner concealed it.

"And your new home is not habitable? I understood you were living there earlier. I mean, being here among your employees and so close to the street may be uncomfortable, possibly even dangerous for Mrs. Townsend if the strikers misbehave. Which no doubt they will. Perhaps you could move back?"

"I'm very comfortable here, Mr. Stone," I said. "But I appreciate your concern."

Barlow's smile was tense.

Mr. Stone took a cigar from his suit coat, squinted at it, smiled, and put it back. "Well, Townsend, I've come on matters which you should put to your partners. We understand you've ordered no replacements. Not wise, sir. But you're new to mining."

"I'm hardly new to business, Hollis, and not at all new to managing men. Nor are our wives ignorant of the situation and of the history of worker demonstrations in this state."

"Yes, the ladies," Stone said. "There is always the possibility of violence. You should consider the ladies."

"I suppose I may speak for the ladies," I said. "But as a point of clarification, when you say 'ladies,' are you including miners' wives?"

Stone smiled as though I'd said something sweet and naïve. "Naturally, we want everyone to be safe. As should the strikers." He directed his gaze to Barlow and spoke in a more insistent tone. "The association believes, Townsend, that the Winkler Mine is setting a bad example. The men will stick together and so must we. The first train of replacements will arrive in a day or two. I suggest you place your order."

"Thank you, but if we decide to use replacement workers, we'll find them ourselves," Barlow said. "To be frank, we like neither the methods nor the results of recruiting agents."

"I see. Well you might consider sending your family out of town for the duration. You'll be in the midst of it, living in this house on the street, close as it is to the railroad tracks."

"I'm sure we will not be in danger from our workers," I said. "Though you may have a point about our proximity to the railroad. I understand that not too many years ago, guards fired machine guns from a train into miners' dwellings. Machine guns, imagine that!"

Hollis Stone looked offended. "That event was highly exaggerated and inaccurately reported. And it happened in the southern part of the state, where miners are incorrigible, you know."

"We'll tolerate no shooting from either side," Barlow said.

"Tolerate?" Stone gave a short laugh. "This is not Sunday school, Townsend. Whatever happens, the miners have brought it on themselves. We are warning our men that if they are not back to work when our replacements arrive, they will have to vacate their houses. Our houses, that is. It will be easier to get everyone back to work if your mine hires replacements like the rest of us.

We will give the men a chance to return to work with no penalties."

I was certain my opinion would have no effect, but I needed to give it. "Mr. Stone, many people believe there would be no hostile relations between operators and workers if you cared more about the men. As human beings, I mean. During the war, our miners' output exceeded everyone's expectations. They kept their word not to strike when coal was needed so desperately. Now they deserve your consideration. At the minimum, a raise in pay."

Stone's smile was tolerant. "Well said, Mrs. Townsend. I much admire women's sentiments, so inspiring with high ideals, and so necessary for bringing up good children. But like most men, I do not find those sentiments practical in business."

Miss Graves or Glory would have given a better retort to the ideas of Hollis Stone, and Virgie and Wanda would likely have spit back stronger language. I tried to keep my voice steady, aware that I must stand up for them as well as for my new friends, Mrs. Greggorio and Mrs. Cox. "Mr. Stone, the world beyond the home depends very much on women, and those who presently run it might profit if they listened to our views."

He rose and reached for his coat. "Townsend, I suggest you take steps to protect your interests. And your family."

CHAPTER 18

Mid-January, the scab train passed through Winkler, slowing down on its way to Barbara Town and Big Bend. I went outside to watch with my neighbors. Men peered from the passenger windows. I pitied their hopeful gaze.

"Lookit that," Mrs. Cox said, pointing to the last passenger car. Like the others, it was full of men, but each of these had a rifle propped at his window.

"More guards," she said. "Making a big show of it."

The cold wind sent us inside, but we both were drawn out not long after that by a parade of sorts in the street.

"Lord help us," Mrs. Cox said. "They're men from the Winkler Mine."

At the far end of the street they crossed the bridge to Barbara Town. "What do you think they're doing?"

"I've no doubt. They're going to join the pickets at the Barbara."

"Will there be a fight?"

"They might do no more than line up and watch the scabs go into the mine, but again, they might give them trouble, depends on how fired up they are. For sure they'll be shouting and carrying on to make the scabs think again, telling them they're riding to their death, saying they're taking food from children, things like that. Cursing and calling names, you can be sure."

Mrs. Greggorio joined us. "Mrs. Townsend, I hope you won't think nothing of it if you see a few extra women and children in houses over here today."

I assured them my husband and I would take no notice. Unless the replacements got back on the train, today the Barbara Town families would be turned out. Virgie and Glory had already offered to shelter a woman and her two small children, and I'd heard rumors that other Winkler families were prepared to do the same, though they knew they might soon be evicted themselves.

"I'll have six extra loaves of bread today," I said, "but I don't know what to do with them."

"We'll take care of that for you," Mrs. Cox said.

Barlow had said he was going to turn a blind eye if families from other towns moved into the few vacancies in Winkler, but those dwellings could not shelter people for long. If the strike dragged on, our company would have to provide housing for replacement workers too. *Provide housing.* Saying it like that felt only slightly better than saying we'd have to kick our miners' families out.

EVERY TIME I LOOKED THROUGH THE FRONT WINDOW THAT afternoon I saw women crossing the bridge to our side of the river with bundles and babies, trailed by older children. I tried to stay busy, kneading bread and playing in the kitchen with Freddy.

The Winkler miners had come back, marched away from the Barbara Mine portal by armed guards. Like Winkler, Barbara Town was private property, but our Main Street had been given status as a state road. Anyone had a right to be there, Glory said.

She and Wanda paid me a brief visit, sharing what they knew along with hopes that we might somehow prevent the worst from happening.

"The association voted to close the school for the duration," Wanda said. "Will told them he owns the building and he'll do with it as he chooses. The association said that's fine and dandy, but their replacement workers came without families, so they see no need to pay the teachers. They said they won't pay the preacher, either, but that don't matter. Soon as the men went out on strike, the preacher flew the coop."

"Barlow has gone to speak with the teachers," I said. "He says there's funds to pay our share through the end of this week, that is if any are willing and able to work for a third of their salary. He believes they cannot. Today will likely be the last day of school."

Glory admired the six loaves of bread cooling on my worktable.

"Mrs. Cox is coming for these," I said. "She's going to deliver them to members of the Ladies' Aid who've taken in Barbara Town families. The union is supposed to bring tents and food supplies by truck, and Milo Karakas has asked if they can set up a distribution center somewhere in town."

"If there's no teaching, they can give out their supplies in the school building," Wanda said. "I'll tell Will. He wants to see what's brought in, to make sure it's not guns. O'course lots of these men already owns guns. Will told the guards not to allow guns on the street or at the shacks they've set up at the portal."

The mention of guns gave us pause. "You might move back up the hill," Wanda said. "Maybe take my kids with you."

I didn't say yes or no. Moving away from the street might be a good idea, but I didn't like it because it had first been suggested by Hollis Stone.

"Restraint," Glory said. "Both miners and guards must demonstrate restraint. What, you don't agree?"

"Oh, sure, we agree," Wanda said. "Hold back, stay calm, well and good. But somebody's gonna have to show them how. It's not like restraint comes natural."

Since what the men might do seemed beyond our control, we changed our talk to what we could do for their women and children. "In a day or so the children will be restless at home," I said. "Especially the ones in houses doubled up. We might hold games in the school, like we did during the Christmas workshop."

Glory liked that idea. "And we'll give them something to eat."

There were hundreds of children. "We'll need a lot of help," I said.

WE EXISTED PEACEFULLY THROUGH JANUARY AND FEBRUARY. Barlow said the miners were too busy keeping warm to cause trouble. When she wasn't helping Glory and Virgie sew children's coats, Luzanna came to help me bake, because with the exception of us, her customers were on strike.

"The miners are all het up, like their strike is a holy crusade," Luzanna said. "I've heard the claim that men who do jobs like theirs should get higher pay than lawyers and bankers, who do their work sitting in safe places. Sometimes I think they're right, but it scares me when they say the world is upside down and they're gonna turn it right-side up. They say all this is for the future. I say that's well and good, but their families have to get along in the present."

I was not an inventive story-teller, but I wracked my brain for any tale that had nothing to do with the present time. She laughed when I told her about Wanda and some boys interrupting the Singing School concert with a fight. I didn't mention the fact that the boys were John Donnelly and his brother. Then I described all the residents of Hester's boardinghouse and Nellie, the sow that had been my pet and companion in my lonely time as Jamie's wife.

"Nellie!" Luzanna roared. "Nellie was my sister's name. She was a bit of a sow herself!" She doubled over. When finally she stopped laughing, she wiped her eyes and said, "I don't know where she got to." Just like that, we were sad again.

⚜

"I'M SORRY, I DON'T THINK I CAN EAT ANYTHING," BARLOW said. I'd cooked grits with a portion of Russell's fresh sausage, but I had no appetite myself. "Will you have coffee?"

"I doubt my stomach can handle it," he said. "I might try peppermint tea, if we have it."

"I think we do. You're not getting sick?"

"It's this business." He pressed his hand to his middle. "It strikes my weakest place."

I poured peppermint tea for both of us, because my stomach was uneasy too. "Are the strikers' demands so unreasonable?"

"They're asking for the same things they've wanted for years, like no more docking their pay for half a ton if there's even a few pieces of slate in a coal cart. That's a reasonable request. They also want a checkweighman. West Virginia law says all miners have a right to employ their own man to work beside the company weighman at the scales. It's a means to keep the operators honest, you see. We've had a checkweighman from the first day, but most operators ignore the law."

Hollis Stone came to mind. It was easy to imagine him ignoring the law.

"It's not easy to do what's right in this state," Barlow said. "Our senators, judges, and a lot of newspaper publishers have financial interests in coal, and the ones who aren't investors have business connections or friendships with those who are. There's independent men here and there, operators and others, but it always feels like we're outnumbered."

"Do the strikers want a raise?"

"A raise is on the list, but Karakas says that's the least of their concerns. They want to trade where they please, and they want to be paid in cash, not scrip. This is also law. It sounds reasonable, doesn't it? And of course they want the union checkoff. That means we'd take dues from every man's pay and send it to the UMW. The union has only a tiny toehold in West Virginia, but unions in other states will put a great effort into this push, both money and manpower. And some will put their lives on the line."

I didn't know what to say. I wished we could jump ahead a few years to a time when all disputes might be resolved.

"I hate it," Barlow said, "but I'm in it now. When the weather warms, the real agitation will start. You and Freddy might go to Elkins. I could get rooms for you there."

"I'd be anxious all the time, not knowing what's happening to you and my friends. And I have work here." I told him about our plans to conduct games for the school children, an endeavor that men like Hollis Stone would think sweet but unimportant.

"Then I'll ask Cox to install shutters on our front windows. If it comes to street fighting, you and Freddy must stay in the back rooms."

"I don't want to shutter our house if the others cannot. Besides, if the men think we expect gunfire, won't they be more likely to keep their own guns handy?"

"You see why I'd like you to go somewhere safe."

"I want my neighbors to be safe, too."

"Randolph believes there are guns in the tent camp, and no doubt quite a few on our side of the street. If we hire replacements..."

We stared at each other. "We should plan for the worst," he said.

"In bad times, we need music," Wanda said. "The teacher told me that, back when the lumber camps shut down. Do you remember Mr. Cooper?"

In my memory, Mr. Cooper had said this because Wanda, the child who claimed nothing ever bothered her, was experiencing a time so bad that she'd refused to sing. She felt abandoned by her mother, who'd said Wanda should not visit her in the brothel any longer. "We got through that bad time," I said.

"So we did. I'm just saying that I'm not the only one who needs music. It's good for everybody. I want to have a sing. We can use the church. You tell your Mrs. Cox to spread the word that it will be tomorrow night. We'll make it for fun only, no preaching and everybody welcome—Catholics too—and we'll abide no talk about the strike. I'll lead some songs and we'll invite others to give us a tune on their guitars and such."

Her enthusiasm made me feel better. "Do you think many will come?"

"Sure they will. If we had a place big enough to do it, I'd get up a dance, and I'm no dancer. But jumping around and stomping to a beat would make us feel good, don't you think?"

"I hope so." Singing and dancing had to be better than exchanging insults.

❧

Wanda was right. Even with short notice, people crowded into the church. In the entire gathering, the only sad face I saw belonged to Alma. Her new young man, the son of the Barbara Mine superintendent, had been sent away by train, destined for a safer location.

Near the end of the evening when the volunteer performers claimed they were sung out, one of our guards stood up and sang a tune that brought tears to my eyes. He had a fine, high voice, sweeter than Grady Malone's. His song was "Danny Boy."

For me, the greatest surprise came not when the audience applauded for the guard to sing again, but when a man with a fiddle came forward from the back of the church and offered to accompany him. That man was Price Loughrie, about whom we'd not heard a word since the death of Wanda's Aunt Ruth. Wanda was never sentimental, but her face looked wet and shiny.

Barlow's arm lay heavily on my shoulder, and by its weight I knew he was affected, too. Price was well-known among the miners, because he'd been checkweighman at the Jennie Town Mine when Barlow worked there, and until last summer, a regular entertainer at Will's Trading Days. The guard sat down after their song, but the crowd would not let Price leave the platform.

Throughout the sing, Freddy had crawled back and forth from my lap to Barlow's, sometimes standing between us on the pew, supported by his father, reveling in the crowd and bouncing to the music. As the evening lengthened, he lay with his head in my lap and his thumb in his mouth, but events were too loud and exciting for sleep. He kept pushing himself up to see, then flopping back down, fussing and squirming. My arms grew weary from the struggle, but my lungs felt renewed, for I'd sung out too, for once without a care that anyone might hear.

Barlow leaned close. "It's past his bedtime. Do you think we should go?"

"Please, not yet."

A husband and wife with banjo and guitar joined Price on the platform, and soon the church was loud with fast music, hand-clapping, and all the stomping Wanda had wanted.

"All right," Wanda said, speaking in a moment that was quiet except for the wails of babies. "This was good. We'll do it again!"

Freddy was bawling now, but I was happy.

CHAPTER 19

"Our days are numbered," Barlow said. We sat close together in the dim light of dawn, warmed by our bed covers and our first sips of coffee. We'd endured two months of the strike and had sold the last of our stockpiled coal. "Randolph does not want to work the mine with ignorant replacements, but he thinks he might scout the southern coal fields for an experienced crew. Price says he's unlikely to find them. Few real miners want to be scabs, and they'll know the work may be temporary."

Price Loughrie had become the trusted contact between the Winkler owners and workers, and a welcome visitor everywhere. He was always well-groomed, with clean fingernails, polished shoes, and a broad-brimmed hat that looked new. His quiet, formal manner made him a favorite of all my friends. Virgie said she wouldn't mind taking care of him, and Charlie admired his high-stepping riding horse. By his own report Price had not touched a drop of liquor since Ruth's death. Barlow said an outsider might think the man was holy, the way miners looked up to him. "When Price is sober he listens more than he talks," Barlow said, "and when he speaks he gives no frivolous advice."

Fires glowing from burn barrels were a common sight at the Winkler Mine portal and also in the strip of land between Main Street and the railroad tracks. Men evicted from Barbara Town sheltered there in tents supplied by the UMW. We'd had snow, but the winter had not been as severe as usual. Price was with the men all day, warming himself at their fires and cheering them with fiddle tunes. Will had given him the key to the school building, and on the coldest nights the Barbara Town miners slept there. For the moment, our workers and their families slept in their homes.

My friends and neighbors talked, sang and laughed, baked and fed the children, but I felt certain that most days their insides were as shaky as mine. And though Barlow's voice and demeanor remained steady, his agitation showed in other ways—indigestion, lapses in speech, leaving the house without notice, and often being unaware that Freddy wanted to crawl onto his lap.

"There's another possibility," he said. "We can walk away from all of this and regain a portion of the money I invested. The railroad has offered to buy us out."

Walk away? Conflicting thoughts struck me at once. How I hated the coal business. How we could rid our bodies of agitation and start over somewhere peaceful. How I'd lose my friends, my home. How we'd leave the Winkler families to the mercy of the new operator. And again, how I hated the coal business. "Would they buy the whole operation or just your share?"

"The offer is for everything the partners own in common. The mining operation, the store goods and company houses, everything except the few properties owned by Will."

He did not say how long he'd known about this offer. Perhaps he'd made his decision. Even with the clear head of morning, this was almost too much to think about. "What do the others say?"

"We've agreed to consider it. So I wanted you to know. Whatever we decide will be hard. I need your understanding."

"It's a dirty trick. The association wants you out."

He took a deep breath.

"Have they offered a good price?"

"Not enough. Randolph says there's great potential in our mine. I don't know, we may decide to let him look for replacements. That would be bad for the families here, but we could try to make it a peaceful transition. On the other hand, if we sell, replacements will come in and railroad guards will turn the families out. I'd want you to leave town ahead of..."

"Chaos," I said. "There's no chance you could grant Winkler miners their demands and let them get back to work?"

"We'd have to leave the association, and you know what that would mean."

It would mean the railroad company refusing to ship our coal.

"We might ditch the association if our miners would agree to wheel the coal to market in barrows," he said. In the low light of morning, I could not see his sad smile, but I heard it in his voice.

"Or in trucks," I said. "It's too bad we don't have a fleet of those trucks that deliver coal to houses in the cities."

"Huh. We've worn ourselves out trying to think of a workable solution. We'd need upwards of a thousand of those house-delivery trucks. A railcar carries about a hundred tons, but I don't know of a truck heavy enough to haul more than a single ton, and those have to be shoveled out. Railcars unload from a chute in the floor, you know."

"What about dump wagons?"

"I've never heard of one that can lift a ton of anything. But wouldn't the other operators burn if a caravan of trucks left here with Winkler coal? I'd love to see their faces, even if we couldn't haul away a significant load."

"If you could get the coal to Elkins, would another railroad company take it from there?"

"You bet they would. The railroad companies hate each other. Someday a truck might be built with a heavy body and a chute like a railcar. If that happens, the railroads will no longer control our transportation."

My coffee had gone cold. "I know you don't want to give up, and I know we can't wait for someday. The union brought food and supplies for the miners in a heavy-looking wagon pulled by a large tractor. Is there a way you could use something like that?"

He passed me his cup and threw back the covers. "Tractors and wagons! May Rose, you've got me thinking. I'm going to wake up Randolph and Will and see if we can stall the railroad offer for another week or two."

I hurried into my robe. "I'll start breakfast."

"Later. Get back in bed and stay warm." He smacked my lips with a kiss and stomped down the stairs so hard that his feet woke Freddy.

CHAPTER 20

R andolph came home after five days of travel, not with
replacements but with a plan to create a vehicle strong
enough to haul coal, an invention he would not talk
about. Barlow said Randolph was like that, never wanting to
discuss an idea until he satisfied himself it would work.

All Barlow knew was that Randolph had something in mind
that had not been tried before. But Randolph also agreed they
should send Price Loughrie to towns in the region, railroad
centers like Elkins and Grafton and smaller burgs along the way
to contact house coal delivery men. "If they're willing to drive
here for it, we'll offer coal at a discount," Barlow said. "Even so,
we can't expect those trucks to save us. I hope Randolph's other
idea is better, but if it doesn't improve our situation, I think we'll
close down. I'd rather see our families leave of their own accord
than be driven out by railroad guards."

"You'd shut down the mine and we'd stay here?"

"We wouldn't be alone. I'm sure Will and Wanda would stay
and perhaps a few others who could make a living for themselves.
The town would be much as it was before we built the mine."

"Except for all those houses, empty."

"Yes. That would feel strange, wouldn't it? But we might open the mine in the future, if the issue resolves and prices are good. Until then, are you ready to be poor?"

"I'm good at being poor. Shutting down sounds better than hiring replacements or selling to another operator. But before that happens I hope we see trucks leave here with Winkler coal. Even if they won't help us in the long run, they'll send a message."

"Randolph doesn't want to get our hopes up about his idea," Barlow said, "and we can't breathe a word to the miners or the association."

☙❦☙

On days when Evie and Alma helped with games in the school, Wanda brought Otis to me. The morning after Randolph's return, she blew in like the fresh air of spring.

"I think they're going to do it," she said, freeing Otis from his sweater. "Break with the association and sign our own union contract. They're in Barlow's office now, talking with Milo Karakas and trying to convince him that our miners won't be deserting the other strikers if they go back to work. I heard Barlow say we can't give them a raise now, because we're gonna be in trouble ourselves, and the men might get no more than a day or two of work each week. But we're making history, Ma!"

She lifted the lid on a pot of beans soaking on my stovetop. "Poor rations in your house too, I see."

"Fortunately we like beans, except for Freddy. I've been feeding him oatmeal and scrambled eggs. "Russell gave me a ham. I'm trying to stretch it."

"Otis will eat beans," she said. "The store got supplies yesterday. It's a relief to be stocked again, because if we break with the association, our goods will have to come by truck. Will's not sure other operators in the association will go on buying from the slaughterhouse if we break away. If they buy meat somewhere else, Charlie and Russell won't have much to do."

"That might be all right. Russell could use a rest." I wished he could retire to his old place, but he'd sold it long ago, and there was no way to reclaim it. His farm was now part of the Big Bend mining camp.

"Well, he's not following Charlie over town anymore. Blanche has that boy all tied up."

I'd stopped worrying about Charlie and Blanche. I only hoped they'd stay out of trouble.

⚜

I HELD MY BREATH ABOUT THE WEATHER, FOR EVEN IF OUR miners returned to work, others would still be camped around burn barrels. As though the heavens pitied them, March came in like a lamb.

The Winkler Mine was not yet back in production, because Milo Karakas was waiting for a decision from the UMW. "Don't tell anyone," Barlow said. "Not Luzanna, not Glory. If word gets out, the association will find some way to block us."

Meanwhile, rumors circulated about other mines. A replacement worker caused an explosion that shut down the Big Bend for a week. We heard stories of replacements robbing company stores before running away from jobs they'd never been prepared to do. Barlow said he'd seen men splashing through the river to get to the state road instead of using the guarded bridge. I'd seen a few men hurrying north on our road, chased by strikers.

Wanda was the only person I knew who was allowed to cross the bridge to Barbara Town. She did that every morning, carrying a mail sack to the depot and bringing home Winkler mail. One sunny afternoon she sent Evie running to my house, looking for Barlow. "Doc Will is on a call," Evie said. "And Charlie's been arrested in Barbara Town."

"Arrested!" I was already stirred up, because Barlow and Randolph had just driven away to attend the association meeting. Today they were going to sever their ties.

"I'll fetch Uncle Russell," Evie said.

"No, please. Stay with Freddy and Otis. I'll find Mr. Loughrie."

My head thumped with every step as I hurried past the smoky fires where Price spent his days with the strikers. Again and again the men said they hadn't seen him. I hoped he hadn't left us in search of liquor. By the time I questioned the last group on the street I'd reached the bridge. Wanda waited on the Winkler side, holding the sack stamped U.S. Mail. I explained why Barlow and Randolph weren't able to come.

"I found out about Charlie when I crossed over a while ago," she said, "Blanche is with him at the Barbara Town Jail. It's in the depot with the post office. They tried to make her go home but she put up a fuss. It's a wonder they didn't lock her up too, but they'd have to put her with the men and it's crowded in there."

"Did they arrest him for trespassing?"

"Not sure," she said. "We'd better sweet-talk these guards."

I didn't feel like sweet talk. When we reached the guards, she held up the mail bag.

"You come through here once already this morning," a guard said.

"Yeah, but the mail window was closed. I didn't get to leave this bag or pick up the one for Winkler." She spoke as rough as the guard, like she was angry with herself.

"Ain't my problem," the guard said.

"'Course it ain't, but this is the U.S. Mail. It's against the law to hold up delivery."

"All right, get on over, but she stays." The guard tipped his head toward me.

"This is my ma, and I need her to carry back the newspapers." Wanda held up her hands. "Come on, do we look like trouble?"

I gave the guard a shy, ladylike smile, not directly in his face, as I'd cautioned Blanche, just what I hoped was a sweet glance before I looked down.

"If you're not back here in a minute I'm gonna come looking for you," he said. "And mind you stay away from them scabs. They don't got manners enough to respect a lady. If you is a lady."

It was no time to take offense. We hurried across the bridge to the depot and its small jail. The mail window was still closed, and except for one guard outside, we saw no others. Inside the depot, Blanche huddled against a wall where she could see Charlie, who paced in a barred room crowded with ragged men. When he saw us, Charlie made his way to the bars. He had a bloody nose and cut knuckles. "Hey, Wanda," he said. "Hey, Ma." Blanche huddled beside us, sniffling. I sniffled too, because it was the first time since his return to Winkler that Charlie had called me anything.

"He got in a fight," Blanche said. "It was 'cause of me, you know. Some o'them men tried to make me go with them."

"Dandy," Wanda said. "How did you and Charlie get past the guards at the bridge?"

"We didn't come over the bridge, we crossed the river on them big rocks and come through the field."

Wanda looked around the depot lobby, which except for us, was still empty. "Who we gotta talk with to get him out?"

Blanche shrugged. "The guards put him there and went away."

I rapped on the mail window and spoke to the man who pushed it up. "Can you direct me to the mine office? I'm carrying a message to the superintendent from my husband, Barlow Townsend. He's one of the Winker Mine owners."

The postmaster yawned. "Want to put the message in the superintendent's box? He'll get it today."

"My husband said I should hand-deliver it. He's on his way to an association meeting. The mine office, please."

"It's around the corner. The superintendent's there. His name is Walker."

I signaled Wanda to follow me. "Let me do the talking," I said, when we left the building.

The guard at the mine office gave us a curious stare as we approached, and I realized that with the exception of Blanche, we might be the only women in Barbara Town. We climbed the steps and let ourselves in.

The superintendent was alone in his office, sitting in a dusty beam of sunlight, wearing a soiled and wrinkled white shirt that was open at the collar. He stood with a blink of recognition and a frown of puzzlement.

I introduced us and asked pardon for interrupting his work, though when we'd entered he might have been day-dreaming.

"My foster son is in your jail," I said. "He's not a miner or a union organizer; he runs the stockyard. He mistakenly crossed into Barbara Town when he was walking in the field with his sweetheart. She says some men here treated her roughly, and he ended up in a fight when he tried to protect her."

Mr. Walker pulled the papers on his desk into a sloppy stack. "That could happen. We've lots of rough types here."

"We've come to take him home, Mr. Walker. Charlie Herff is his name. He's Dr. Herff's brother. This is Dr. Herff's wife. Our husbands have gone to the association meeting, or they would be here personally. I think they'll be relieved, when they come home, to learn you've helped us take care of this misunderstanding."

"The doctor's son, you say?"

"No, the doctor's brother. He's my foster son. He's somewhat limited in speech, due to an accident, but we're all very fond of him, Mr. Townsend too, of course."

"I see." He waved his hand. "Wait a minute and I'll tell the guard to turn him out. Your son should know it's not safe to be over here."

"We will impress the need to observe boundaries. Good luck with your work, Mr. Walker. And give our best to your family."

Again he tried to arrange the stack of papers. "They're away at present."

"Yes, very wise, but the separation must be lonely for you. I'm sorry."

Outside, we followed the guard to the jail. "Ma, you can really lay it on," Wanda said. "Wait till I tell Barlow."

"I do feel sorry for that man. And you should find some other way to fetch the mail."

⚜

WE MIGHT NEVER HAVE GOTTEN CHARLIE RELEASED FROM JAIL if the superintendent had known the results of that afternoon's association meeting.

"We gave our notice," Barlow said, stopping at the house on his way to an evening of office work.

"What did they say?"

"Not much. They laughed and blew their cigar smoke. The railroad representative told us to come around when we were ready to sell out. I'm certain our leaving the association confirmed what they've always thought—that we've no idea how to run a mine."

"They didn't say you couldn't use their railroad?"

"It wasn't necessary."

"So how...?"

"One problem at a time," he said.

⚜

WORD SPREAD QUICKLY FROM MILO KARAKAS TO THE MEN. The Winkler owners had come to terms with the UMW. Our miners were going back to work.

Mrs. Cox and Mrs. Greggorio came that evening and delivered their thanks. "The men are stubborn. They won't say thank you for something they think is theirs by right," Mrs. Cox said. "You don't need to tell your husband that part. Just say we're all grateful. And we are, the men too."

It took only a glance through the front window to catch the excitement at the burn barrels. Men slapped each other's shoulders and passed what might be their last bits of tobacco, even though for most of them the strike was not settled.

Virgie, Glory and Luzanna arrived to hear why Charlie had been jailed and how he'd been freed, making me realize I'd forgotten to tell Barlow.

"These are bad times to be walking over town," Virgie said. "Maybe Blanche and Charlie would be better off if they cabined up together."

Glory looked horrified. "You don't mean that."

"Sure I do. We know how Blanche is—she'll devote herself to a man, and if she's not got a particular one, she keeps looking. Charlie may be strange, I don't know, maybe he always was or maybe it's from the beating he took. But I'll bet he functions like any other man, and he's kind, ain't he? I'd say he likes her. May Rose, what do you think?"

I had too many thoughts. "They couldn't just live together; our good deacons won't tolerate anyone living in sin, not even... I mean, they'd be knocking on his door and preaching hellfire until they got him and Blanche to the church. And would marriage keep them safe? Besides, none of us knows what Charlie wants." I had no idea how Russell would react if Blanche tried to move in.

"Put it to Wanda," Virgie said. "If you don't want to, I will."

Glory and I exchanged a satisfied glance. Of the three of us, Wanda was the one most protective of Charlie.

Pleased with Virgie's suggestion, we went on to share our relief that the Winkler miners were going back to work. I said nothing about the mine leaving the association nor our problem of getting coal to market. By the time my friends left, a small wrinkle on Glory's brow suggested she had begun to wonder about it.

Near bedtime, I heard the echo of rifle shots. Barlow had not come home for supper, and I paced for the next hour, periodically going outside to look down the street. Judging from fast-moving shadows near the burn barrels, something was happening in the tent camps.

When Barlow hurried through the door, I hugged him before he could take off his coat. He took my hand and led me to the kitchen. "We should keep away from the street and sleep in the back bedroom with Freddy tonight."

He gripped my hand as though I might run to the street to see what was wrong. "Barbara Mine guards have come into Winkler. They're raiding the tent camps."

"Because our miners are going back to work?"

"No, because someone shot the Barbara superintendent."

"Good Lord, Mr. Walker?"

"That's the one. They claim the killer got away to our side of the river." For a moment, a volley of distant gunshots stopped our talk.

"Who's shooting?"

"I'm not sure."

"Mr. Walker is dead?"

"So I believe."

With a company man deliberately shot, the mine operators would bring more guards to protect themselves. It was possible that nobody would be safe. Barlow and I stood in the kitchen with our arms around each other as shouts and curses rose on the street. Someone pounded on our front door. "Sit down and stay here," Barlow said.

I could not sit down. I stood in the doorway between the kitchen and front room as he went out and faced a group of men. I heard him say, "What's this about?" Then he stepped outside and closed the door.

If I could not see, I had to hear. I crept to the door and stood with my ear against it.

One voice was so loud I might have heard it from the kitchen. "Give way! We're searching every house."

Barlow shouted in return: "Not in Winkler. This is private property."

The others grumbled. "Step aside. We got police work to do."

"You're not police," Barlow said. "You and your guns have no business here. If you think a search of Winkler houses is necessary, you'll have to bring the sheriff. And a warrant."

I wanted to run upstairs and protect Freddy, but I was afraid Barlow's command might not be enough to stop a mob of angry men. It didn't matter that I'd be no help; I couldn't leave him.

"Mr. Townsend!" A new voice raised above the others. "Sorry for this disturbance. You men stop bothering Mr. Townsend. He's one of the Winkler Mine owners."

I pulled back the window curtain. Three men stood in the street. I could not distinguish their faces but I saw their rifles. When the Barbara Mine guards swung their own guns toward the newcomers, I clutched the curtain so tightly that it started to tear from the rod.

A Barbara guard turned back to Barlow. "Owner, are you? Then you can give us permission to search Winkler."

One of the men in the street took a step closer. "We're the law on this side of the river. Mr. Townsend, you'd best go back inside your house. We wouldn't want you to catch a bullet meant for one of these donkeys."

Yes, I thought, come inside; we'll go to the back of the house as you said we should. I waited for the door to open, but it did not. By now the three Winkler guards had been joined by a dozen or more others, a few in miners' caps.

"If there's damage to life or property here, we'll sue your employer," Barlow said. "Confine yourself to Barbara Town. No one is going to search Winkler houses but the sheriff. If he brings a warrant."

Outnumbered, the intruders gave up. I opened the door and watched with Barlow as Winkler guards herded them past jeering miners at the burn barrels.

"I need to talk with Will and Randolph," Barlow said. "This murder may be all the governor needs to send in his new special police."

The shaking I'd kept under control while I watched at the window now caught up with me. At Paint Creek, soldiers in the West Virginia National Guard had been directed to fight on the side of the operators. I hoped the sheriff would come soon. He was an old friend of Will and Price Loughrie.

When Barlow left, Mrs. Cox knocked on my door. "Dearie, are you all right? Those men pushed right into my house and searched every nook, turned over the beds and rummaged through the closets. They did others the same way. Wouldn't even say what it was all about."

"We're fine," I said. "Did they hurt anyone?" It was easy to imagine miners resisting the search.

"No, praise God. Some of our men has been living across the way in the tent camps, keeping faith with the Barbara miners you know. In my house the thugs found nobody but us women and kids. I saw Mr. Townsend go down the street. Would you want to bring the boy and stay with us till he comes home?"

"Freddy's asleep," I said. "We'll be all right." I'd never been less certain.

CHAPTER 21

The murder of the Barbara superintendent heightened the tension in our house, though we did not speak of it again, I suppose because it felt so personally threatening. More than ever I wanted the tent camps to go away, afraid they might be harboring too many men with violent natures.

"Go up to our house today," Barlow said the next morning. "See if you think it's suitable for us to move in." This time I agreed it might be a good idea.

Today our miners were going back to work, and school was to resume with only half the teachers. The lower grades would attend in the morning and the upper in the afternoon. It should have been a happy day, but my fearful mood deepened when a guard arrived to escort Barlow to his office.

Since her son had been one of the carpenters, I invited Mrs. Cox to see the progress on our house. When we met on the street, children were walking toward school. Barbara Town guards were visible at the tipple and rail sidings, protecting their coal and cars.

"Surely it won't help the strikers if they destroy property," I said.

"Some men have hair triggers," she said. "It takes nothing to set them off. And some of them has built up so much hate for the owners they don't care what happens to themselves. It's a bad thing, but there you have it."

"My husband said the sheriff will come today. I hope if anyone knows who shot Mr. Walker, they'll give him up."

"I'm praying for that," Mrs. Cox said.

I entered our house on the hillside with anxious feelings, sorry it was so big and sorry we'd put so much into it when our future here depended on getting Winkler coal to market. But Mrs. Cox admired it, top to bottom. The house felt warm because the workers had kept a fire in the new furnace to help dry the plastered walls. Upstairs, sun glinted through new windows.

"Looks like you only need your wood trim, your stair railing, and a bit of cleanup," Mrs. Cox said. "I'll miss having you as my neighbor."

"I'll be just three streets away," I said.

She smiled as though she knew my sad secret. Without rail freight, the mine would soon have to shut down, and she and her son would leave with the others.

҈

ONCE AGAIN OUR FRONT DOOR SHOOK FROM POUNDING FISTS, this time in the middle of the night. I watched from the top of the stairs as Barlow parted the window curtain, then opened the door, bringing in a stronger odor of smoke than normally hung in the valley.

Voices from the street shouted, "Fire! Fire!"

Fire in the mine, fire in town? Barlow passed me on the stairs, pulling off his nightshirt as he ran. "It's our house on the hill!"

He left while I was struggling into my shoes. Freddy was already crying for attention. I dressed him in day clothes, panicky that we might all have to run for our lives. But there was only one house burning, a brick house that sat alone on the highest street, its shooting flames unlikely to spread to any others. The horse-drawn fire wagon rumbled uphill and the street became noisy with shouts of men.

Mrs. Cox and Mrs. Greggorio let themselves into the house and watched with me at the kitchen window. Frightened by the red sky and sickened by the biting odor of destruction, I stayed on my feet only with the aid of my hands on a chair back and the comforting press of these women at my sides. I nodded when they pointed to the shadows of men passing buckets of water up three streets, though even the men must know their effort was useless. Then my other friends arrived—Luzanna, Virgie and Glory, Wanda and Piney. They put water to boil on the stove, held Freddy, settled him in bed, and when the flames died to smoke, made me sit down. Nobody commented on the fire, how hot it seemed to burn, how sad it was to lose all that work. None of them said how lucky we were not to be living there at the time. I didn't cry. I thought of my husband, how disappointed he'd be, and what I must say.

"We haven't lost everything."

Everyone murmured agreement. I think they would have agreed with anything I said.

A DRIZZLING RAIN PERSISTED FOR THE NEXT TWO DAYS. I COULD not bear to look out the back windows, for smoke continued to rise from the ruins of my house. I also hated our view of the street, where striking miners huddled under their oilskins just a few paces from Barbara Mine guards and guns.

"We'll build it back," Barlow said. "Or build on another site, wherever you want."

I said nothing for fear of revealing that at present I only wanted to be where I did not see guns and charred brick walls. I

did not cry until Russell and Charlie brought our picnic table and
set it in the small back yard of our company house.

Having lived with awareness that anything could happen did
not make a disaster any easier to bear. I told myself that people
recovered from loss, but in the following days I was overcome by
a sense of doom. I'd never before been afraid that my husband
might not come safely home from work. The only consolation
was that I was not alone. From the owners to the smallest child,
every life in our mining towns was disrupted, and many were
desperate.

I felt worse when rumors emerged from the tent camp that
the fire had been deliberately set. "Maybe not," Barlow said. "In
bad times like these, any accident is likely to be attributed to an
evil plot."

I urged him to be careful each time he left the house, though I
didn't know what precautions might be required. I tried not to
reveal myself with excessive clinging when he returned. Wisely,
Barlow avoided all talk of where we might live. For days we spoke
only of ordinary things.

My friends stopped to see me every day, and women I didn't
know appeared at our door with gifts of condolence, baked goods
and household items like crocheted doilies and hooked rugs. I
asked the visitors about the health of their families, and having
discovered a good use for gossip, passed these safe topics in idle
chatter to my husband. But we could not for long keep silent
about the problems and events surrounding us.

Piney did the most to set my feelings right. She and Simpson
had invited us for Sunday dinner, and afterwards Simpson and
Barlow decided to walk up to our house. "You can leave Freddy
with me if you want to go along," Piney said.

We were sitting on her back porch, watching Freddy pick
dandelions and Blanche's children play marbles. A Sunday hush
shrouded the town, and the children had been warned to play
quietly or they'd have to go inside. From where we sat, it was

possible to see one corner of our house on the hill, a view that did not show much destruction.

"I'm afraid I couldn't look at it without crying," I said.

She clenched her lips in sympathy. "Simpson feels as bad as if the place was his own. I shouldn't tell, but he cried over it, and I never before seen a man cry. I'm glad him and Barlow's gone up there together. The more they get used to how it is, the better they'll feel. You will, too."

With a yell, Robert pried a marble from his younger brother's fist, and Piney left the porch and pulled him back to sit on the step. "Seems like me and Simpson has to take turns at being the strongest. When one of us is down, the other has to show a hopeful side."

Piney never criticized, but her words let me see I could be helping my husband. Above the blackened brick, the sky was calm and blue. Tiny green leaves speckled the dark branches of bushes and trees, and the air was pleasantly warm. I'd find no more hopeful atmosphere for facing the truth. I spoke quietly to Piney. "If you take Freddy inside, he won't see me go."

She rose right away, calling, "Cookies!" The children threw down their marbles and scampered to the porch. Trying to keep up, Freddy fell to his knees. I started to go to him, but Piney scooped him up and carried him through the door.

I tried to prepare myself as I walked up the street, but when the house came fully in view, I felt like I'd entered a room to view a friend in a burial box. Though it was hard to believe anyone would enjoy seeing it, there'd been so many curious visitors that Barlow had arranged for mine guards to rope off the property. At intervals, wooden signs staked in the ground warned DANGER and KEEP OUT.

Barlow and Simpson came from the far side of the house, paused and bent their heads in solemn conversation. When I drew near, they stopped talking, and Simpson tipped his hat and left. Barlow held out his hand. Holding it was a comfort.

"You won't try to go inside," I said.

"Not yet."

He guided me at a safe distance around the house to view the charred wooden porches, the shattered windows and the roof that had fallen in. Later I might be able to take in more detail, but for now I could do no more than glance.

I stopped at the garden fence and swung open the gate. This view was more promising, for our backs were to the house. "I've been trying to decide where to make our garden this summer," I said. "I think it would be better here, don't you? There's more room for it, and we know the soil is good."

"Are you sure? A garden here won't be handy to our house. I mean the house where we are now."

Turning around, I looked past the ruins to the valley below, the river and railyard, tent camps and the tin roofs of Winkler houses. "Barlow, it's all right. Our house will always be the place where we're together. And I'll manage going back and forth from there to this garden. Freddy can help." We smiled at the thought.

"So." He took a deep breath. "What shall we do?"

"We don't have to decide now." I was afraid to ask what we could afford. Besides, too much was unsure.

My visit to the house got me out of the doldrums and helped me look ahead. I think it helped Barlow, too, or maybe it was only that he no longer worried about me.

I consoled Blanche when she sat in our front room and cried for our loss. "We'll be fine," I said. "Look, we weren't hurt in the fire, and we have most of our clothing and furniture."

"It was so nice up there," Blanche said.

"It was. But you've made me feel better."

She dried her eyes. "I have?"

"It's good to know how much people care." It was true.

She stood and hugged me. "Charlie cares too. I just love him," she said.

WITH NO NEW PREACHER ASSIGNED TO OUR CHURCH, PRICE Loughrie presided over the Sunday service, reading scripture, accompanying hymns on his fiddle and offering prayers. So far he hadn't preached. Barlow said he hadn't gained confidence to do it without first downing a shot or two of whiskey.

I was so impressed by the simplicity and peace of Price's service that I asked Barlow to invite him home for dinner. He was always a pleasant guest, and I needed positive thoughts.

At dinner Price ate slowly and complimented everything, though our meal was only what I could put together after church —fried ham, potatoes, brown beans, sauerkraut and a pudding made the day before. I'd sent Freddy to Luzanna's house so we could have an adult dinner and not one dominated by a child who chewed his fingers along with whatever else was in his mouth.

With the exception of his addiction to liquor, Price had no observable deficiencies. In fact, he stood out in every gathering as a man favored with many gifts. Chief among these was humility, perhaps in extreme. He thought he was nothing.

"Price, many of us hope you'll settle in Winkler," Barlow said, after both men declared they could eat no more.

Price slowly folded his napkin and laid it beside his plate. "I seem to have trouble staying in one place, but I think I'll be here as long as I'm needed."

"I haven't had a chance to say how sorry I am about Ruth," I said.

He thanked me. "I didn't deserve her. I ran away from her once, well twice, for at the end I couldn't stand to see her put in the ground. She was the strongest woman I ever knew, except for that one weakness, and she saved my life. Your husband did too."

"I don't remember any such occasion," Barlow said, "though having you at the Jennie Town Mine saved my sanity." He smiled across the table. "As did my letters from this girl. But Price, you mean a lot to the men. If they could, they'd make you governor."

Price looked astonished. "Then I'd really have to run away." He looked down at his folded hands. "I couldn't save Ruth. Barlow took me home to her when I got so bad on whiskey that I stopped eating. I was ashamed to go, but he took me anyway. She saved me, but I couldn't do the same for her."

According to Wanda, the damage to Ruth's liver had begun long before she knew Price. But I knew how feelings regularly blocked the truth. Maybe Price knew that too, which would explain why he worked so well with the strikers.

"So about our fire," Barlow said. "I'm told there are rumors in the camps."

I wanted to know, yet I was sorry Barlow had turned to this subject.

"Men in the camps claim your house burned too fast," Price said. "They're outside a good part of the night, watching for guards up to no good and keeping warm at the barrels. They said the fire didn't start slow and natural, it kind of exploded. They showed me empty gasoline cans someone found in the brush nearby."

"We had no gas cans at the house," Barlow said.

Our dinner conversation had been marked with friendship, reason and good will, but now I felt bitter with suspicion. Was the fire the work of a lone vandal, a firebug, or a conspiracy? Was the culprit still near? It was hard not to suspect the worst. "Do the men have someone to accuse?"

"They say they don't know," Price said. "There's no ill feeling toward you or the Winkler mine by any of the strikers. The favored opinion is it was done by Barbara Mine guards or one of their scabs."

"We'll never be able to prove it," Barlow said.

"They said if they find who he was, they'll take care of him for you."

"I hope you advised against that."

"I offered the opinion that you would like information to take to the sheriff."

"Exactly right."

"They gave the sheriff the name of Mr. Walker's murderer," Price said. "Of course the man is long gone."

Barlow straightened in surprise. "I'm glad to hear it. I mean I'm glad they gave him up."

I hoped the man was far away. I'd worried one of us might be his next target.

"Milo Karakas has been a good influence," Price said. "Also, we don't need to worry that the governor's special police will arrive and heat everything up. At this point, the special police exist only on paper. It will take months for them to organize."

Their talk turned to the progress of the strike against association mines. "The warm weather is making the men restless," Price said. "Milo is trying to keep them calm. He tells them there's hope the association will soon come to terms with the UMW, for most of their scabs are wastrels or unfit for work. Best thing the scabs do is to give the operators an appreciation for men who know their jobs and don't gum up the works. We hear the mines are losing money."

"We're losing money too," Barlow said. "But I hope you're right about the association being ready to settle. The operators have been set in their beliefs. It's hard to do something a new way."

Price lifted his coffee cup in salute. "I'll drink to that."

TWO WEEKS AFTER OUR MINERS WENT BACK TO WORK, strange-looking vehicles appeared in Winkler. These were large tractors pulling wagons of the type I'd described to Barlow, but the tractors and wagons were connected by thick hoses, and the wagons had steel beds. The new combination included a feature I'd not heard of before: hydraulics.

Randolph was visibly proud. "I contacted an acquaintance who made heavy trucks and wagons for the war. After the armistice he had a factory full of unsold vehicles. When I told him what we needed, he began to tell me about an inventor who was using hydraulics to lift a wagon bed. The two were eager to experiment on heavier vehicles they could sell to a new market, like ours."

As best I understood it, hydraulics involved putting fluids such as oil under pressure great enough to push up a cylinder with enough force to tilt a wagon full of coal. Randolph introduced us to the hydraulics engineer, who'd come along to make sure everything worked when our coal unloaded in Elkins. So far he and the truck manufacturer had cobbled together only two of these vehicles, but they were supplemented in the next days by scores of small house-coal delivery trucks.

Our new kind of transportation was far less efficient than railcars, but as I'd hoped, it sent a message. Men in the tent camps turned out to cheer the trucks on their way.

Price stopped at our house and watched the procession with us. "Miners know more about association politics than you might think," he said.

CHAPTER 22

Warmer weather drew people outside, revealing the numbers of Barbara Town women and children who'd spent the winter months doubled up with Winkler families. On sunny afternoons they strolled along Main Street, often joined by their men from the tent camps. The families' joy seemed created for the occasion, an attempt to strengthen their will to hang on, or a last effort to show the association they'd never give up.

One afternoon, Mrs. Cox knocked at my front door with two women who looked vaguely familiar. "These ladies would like to visit a minute," she said. She introduced them as Mrs. Ivan and Mrs. Everson. My neighbors and I usually visited in the kitchen, but not knowing these women, I invited them to sit in the front room.

"They're from Barbara Town," Mrs. Cox said.

"I see. I hope your strike will soon be settled. With terms good for everyone."

Mrs. Ivan nodded. "There's hope for that." She twisted her hands in her lap. "It's been a hard time."

We nodded in solemn agreement.

"You're a good person."

My face heated. "I hope so. We all have to try."

"Things don't go unnoticed, like how you and some others have kept bread on our tables, fed the kids and all." Mrs. Ivan thrust out her chin, like she was defending herself.

I knew her then. She was the woman who'd called me evil.

"We've come to say we're sorry," the other woman said. "About your baby buggy."

I hadn't seen the buggy since Barlow had wheeled it away during the epidemic, full of food and blankets.

"It's out by your door," Mrs. Ivan said. "One of our men whittled new spokes, and we sewed up a new cushion and gave the wicker a bit of polish. It's not as good as new, but me and my friends will try to make it up to you, soon as we're on our feet again."

Mrs. Cox's eyes said she hoped I'd understand that this visit was hard for them.

"Thank you for finding the buggy—and for fixing it," I said. "I'm glad to have it again." None of us mentioned the deed for which the women wanted to make up.

⚜

A MONTH AFTER BARLOW AND HIS PARTNERS SETTLED WITH THE UMW, the association granted a similar contract to their miners, the tents came down, and the strikers went back to work. Then Hollis Stone presented a new proposition to Barlow and his partners.

"They want us back in the association," Barlow said. He'd saved this news for the calm, early morning time when it was easier to speak of difficult things. We were sitting in bed with our morning coffee, waking up with the twitter of dawn birds and a breeze through the open window. "And the railroad still wants to buy our mine."

I was surprised. "What was your response?"

"That we'd discuss everything."

"And?"

"We haven't been able to talk about it. I think we'll end up rejoining the association. Our company is sunk in debt, but I don't think any of us is ready to think about selling."

"Is it a better offer than before?"

"Surprisingly, yes."

"Then I suppose at some time you'll have to talk about it, at least so you can say yes or no."

He set his coffee cup on the bedside table, pulled up the covers and laced his fingers through mine. "We've put a lot of ourselves into this mine and the town. I wanted to know how you feel about continuing as we are. It's been harder than we expected."

"It's been a hard winter, but not my worst."

"And now I could make everything easier for you. So, should I sell out? We could start a new life in Grafton or anywhere. I could retire and take care of you and Freddy."

His mention of retirement pushed my thoughts in a new direction. I'd seen how the mine business wore him down, almost as much as if he'd been digging coal. I wondered if he was asking for a rest.

"We should sit down with Randolph, Will, and Wanda," I said. "Whenever they're ready to talk."

"It's going to be a sore subject. Randolph is passionate about the mine, and Will feels the same way about this town."

❃

"I THINK EVERY THIRD WOMAN IN TOWN IS EXPECTING," VIRGIE said. We were all at her house except Wanda, who'd gone with Will to help deliver a baby, and Blanche, who'd lost interest in our gathering. Today we were hemming receiving blankets and sewing infant undershirts.

"I never thought I'd say this, for I always wanted a child of my own, but now I'm glad to be too old for that," Piney said. "I barely get through my day with Blanche's kids. What would I do with another baby?"

I hoped Blanche would give her no more. If Piney worried about Blanche and Charlie, she never said, but it seemed impossible to keep them apart. I didn't like to think what they might get up to, but so far we'd seen no evidence of the kind of activity that resulted in a baby.

Luzanna paused her foot on the sewing machine treadle. "It's always a surprise to me, when the coats come off in spring, to see how many women are in the family way. And I'm like Piney, always relieved I'm not one of them."

Virgie winked. "In the spring we see what was going on under the covers those cold winter nights. And o'course this year all the men here had time on their hands. There must have been a lot of going back and forth from them tents, which was probably a good thing. Nothing tames a hostile spirit like regular eruptions of love, if you know what I mean."

Once again Virgie had shocked us into laughter. She would have hooted if I'd taken this moment to reveal my own suspicions, but I wasn't ready to tell even Barlow that I'd missed my monthly and had my first episode of morning sickness.

"May Rose," Glory said, "I hope you don't tell Uncle Barlow the things Virgie says."

My face was still hot with embarrassment. "Glory, I couldn't say them even to myself."

"Aw, it gets easier with practice," Virgie said. "I don't say such things in mixed company, and not to anyone I don't know, or to women who've not been with a man. Well, there's Glory, but I think the more she hears about all that the better off she'll be. Anyway, she's got some news. Randolph Bell paid us a nice visit."

We all stopped sewing.

Glory shook her head. "There's no news."

"But he asked if you'd consider him, I heard it," Virgie said.

We spoke almost in unison: "And you said?"

"I said I would consider, because it seemed cruel to reject him outright, and he had such a pitiful look on his face."

Virgie ended our suspense. "But she's not given it a minute's thought. She tells me she'll refuse him."

"He's a good man," I said. "And you know how Barlow and Will admire him."

"I like Randolph, and I'm aware of his good qualities. But there's no attractiveness to him. If I married him I'd have ugly daughters with poorly-set teeth."

"Maybe your girls would look like you," Piney said. "Or you'd have all boys."

Virgie smoothed and folded another infant shirt and added it to our basket. "For sure any of their kids would be clever. I think he'd give her anything she wanted. Trouble is, Glory don't know what she wants."

"I do know what I want, at least for now. I want to go to Richmond with Virgie and design dresses for rich ladies. I shouldn't have given him hope."

"Absence makes the heart grow fonder," Virgie said.

Glory frowned. "And out of sight is out of mind."

I did not laugh with the others, thinking how Barlow would hate Glory's plans.

I'D AGREED TO PRESENT GLORY'S AMBITIONS TO BARLOW, AND I did my best that evening as I cleared away the dishes. "She's lived in Richmond before. She's familiar with the city, and has friends who will help them get settled."

"When she lived in Richmond she had her brother as chaperone," Barlow said.

I shared his apprehension, but her ambition reminded me of Hester, and it put me on her side. "Will wasn't much of a chaperone. If you remember, her letters said he was seldom at home. She had her own studies and made her own friends. We really knew nothing about her life there, and I suspect Will didn't know much, either."

"But associating with Virgie? She'll attract the wrong kind of people."

"They'll attract women who love fashion and well-made dresses. Your sister raised Glory to be an independent woman. We have to let her go."

"I doubt you'd say that so easily if she were our daughter."

"I'm sure I would not."

His eyes narrowed. "Why are you smiling?"

"I'm remembering how opposed you were when your sister adopted Glory. And now you consider yourself her father."

While I washed the dishes, he'd been sitting at the table, and now he took my hand and pulled me onto his lap. "So if one daughter must go away, maybe I should have another." He bent his head to my shoulder. "Dear girl, I've heard you throwing up. I'm sorry you're sick, but I think it's wonderful news."

It was wonderful news, but it increased my uncertainty about everything. "Let's not tell anyone," I said, "until we know all is well."

"Have you spoken with Wanda recently?"

"Not since school let out. Evie's been minding Otis, and Wanda is often called out as a midwife."

"Will says they're expecting again."

My first reaction was a selfish worry for myself. "I hope she won't think I should take care of her new one and mine too."

"If she asks you to keep another baby, I'll answer for you," Barlow said. "I know how you are with Wanda."

CHAPTER 23

W hen Barlow and Simpson met in our kitchen to discuss tearing down the wreckage of our house, they got sidetracked by another subject. Simpson folded and unfolded his thick, hairy fingers on our tabletop. "Blanche wants to get married. She says Charlie's willing, but I'd like them to have your blessing. Will's too, of course."

This news came as no surprise. I only hoped Charlie was not being hoodwinked. To save Simpson's feelings, I chose my words carefully. "Glory and Wanda think Charlie and Blanche would be better off if they settled somewhere together. And I agree. But you know how they attract trouble. I'm sorry, I don't mean to criticize your daughter."

Simpson nodded. "It's all right, I know how she is."

"She's a good girl, and Charlie's good hearted, but since his accident he's prone to violence. We don't know how he might react if she made him angry. Russell keeps him in line."

"There may be a solution," Simpson said. "Lucie keeps talking about going home to the farm, but we know she can't live alone. She's quite attached to Blanche, and I think she would accept Charlie if he wanted to live there. Blanche has never been good about doing any chore on her own, but she'll work for a boss who keeps after her, like Lucie. And she's eager to please Charlie." Simpson's pale eyebrows raised hopefully. "Russell could go, too."

At first I hated the idea, because at Lucie's farm Charlie would be farther from me. But he'd also be farther from everyone, safe from trouble. "You don't think Lucie would try to come between Blanche and Charlie, or provoke him in some way?"

Simpson smiled. "She might try, but I think she kind of sees how it is with Charlie. Piney nearly faints when she sees how Lucie caters to him."

"I suppose Russell and Charlie could manage a few head of cattle and horses. They'd earn their way."

"It's time to plow," Barlow said. "If they're going to go, they should go soon."

Simpson and I thought so, too.

That evening, Barlow brought Russell and Charlie to the house for ground steak and gravy, Russell's favorite.

I began to question Charlie as soon as the food was on his plate, because I wasn't sure he'd stay when he heard what I had to say, especially if he'd already eaten his fill. "Charlie, do you want to marry Blanche?"

He frowned like he didn't understand.

"That's what her wants," Russell said.

I redirected the subject. "Russell, you know Lucie Bosell's place."

"It's all right," he said.

"You and Charlie could have your own herd there."

He looked up from his plate. "The old woman's give it up?"

"She wants to go back. And she wants you and Charlie—and Blanche—to go along. You can live and work there."

"Live there." Russell was quiet while he chewed. Then he stretched his arm and forked another patty of ground steak across the table to his plate. "She's got a mighty small house."

"Simpson will help you build an addition. Or a separate place. If Charlie and Blanche get married."

Russell chewed. "I ain't gonna work for Lucie Bosell."

"You don't have to work for anyone but yourself. And for Charlie."

Russell nodded toward Charlie, who was busy scraping potatoes and gravy to the edge of his plate. "If the boy goes."

"I'll be going," Charlie said. He hadn't looked up once during Russell's talk, and these were his only words on the matter.

In the absence of a licensed preacher, Price Loughrie read the marriage service in the church for Blanche and Charlie the following Sunday afternoon. Glory and Virgie had remade one of their dresses, exciting Blanche with the imitation pearls on its bodice and on the cap that held her veil. Wanda whispered that Charlie had smartened up of his own accord, shaving his beard and picking out a new shirt, trousers and new high-heeled boots in the store. Though the church was empty of everyone but family, Charlie frowned and glanced about like he expected an ambush. Russell had declined to attend, mumbling he should get on to the farm with their horses.

As soon as Price declared them man and wife, Charlie took Blanche's hand and bolted for the door. Outside, we found them waiting in Lucie's farm wagon. As soon as Piney and Simpson helped Lucie onto a padded seat, Charlie flicked the reins. Lucie grabbed her hat with one hand and the seat rail with the other. Blanche waved, but Charlie did not look back.

Wanda slid her arm around my shoulder. "They'll be all right, Ma."

THROUGH DAYS OF NAUSEA, I WATCHED BARLOW STRUGGLE with his thoughts, and I caught him watching me, both of us waiting for the other to comment in favor of staying or selling. He said his partners still weren't ready to talk about it.

Will said my exhaustion could be lingering effects of influenza, complicated by the new pregnancy. With spring winds, I developed a constant cough, due, I thought, to coal dust. My neighbors washed grime from their front windows every week and rinsed their front steps every day. When I felt too weak to do anything but care for Freddy, Luzanna washed mine.

She was helping me clean the kitchen when she began to speak of her newest concern. "My girl is worrying me to death," she said.

"Alma or Emmy?"

"Of course it's Alma. Emmy's a momma's girl—she'll be hanging on to me forever. No, Alma's been blue ever since that Walker boy was sent away, the one whose pa was killed. He wrote her once from some place in Pennsylvania, and she wrote back, but then he wrote no more. She's disgusted with all the men and boys in Winkler. She says if she stays here she'll be an old maid for sure. And now she's got this idea in her head that she should go to Richmond with Virgie and Glory."

I was as apprehensive as Luzanna. "Maybe Alma is too young to be..."

"On her own and around Virgie, I know. But she's kind of prissy. I've told her the kind of things Virgie says, not her exact words, of course. She thinks Virgie is scandalous. It's Glory she admires. So she hopes you'll sound them out about her going along. She's got this idea to go to college, you see, and to earn her keep by cleaning and doing their laundry. Or if that's not possible, she thinks they might help her find a place to live and work. I think she's way too young, but a ma don't always think straight when her kids decide it's time to bolt."

"I'm sure Glory and Virgie would love to have her, but I hate to see her go. It seems like everyone's leaving."

"Not us," Luzanna said.

"Not us." I felt deceitful, for Barlow and I had not decided. "I'll speak with Glory and Virgie about Alma."

THE MORE I COUGHED, THE MORE BARLOW TALKED OF GETTING me away from the coal dust that blew from the rail cars. "I'll do whatever you want," he said. "If the others won't sell, someone might buy my share."

I wanted to leave this place but not my friends, and not the ones who called me "Ma." This time if I moved away I couldn't take them with me, for they had their own lives. I feared that Luzanna would not do as well without us. I was sure I would not do as well without her.

Virgie and Glory, who did not know about the railroad's offer to buy the mine, thought my distraction had to do with whether or not to rebuild the house. "You could move into my place," Virgie said. "Being away from Main Street, it's easier to keep clean, and we've got the bathroom now. You could add another room."

We'd gathered again in Virgie's parlor to work on dresses for Alma's new life as a student in Richmond. Our conversation did not linger long on my house decision, for Virgie wanted to talk about something more interesting: Glory and Randolph Bell.

"We've not moved from sight and already the man is showering Glory with letters," Virgie said.

We turned to see Glory's playful smile. "He writes in a beautiful hand," she said. "And quite lyrical for an engineering type. But never fear, I'm going to Richmond."

While we enjoyed teasing Glory, I wondered privately if Richmond might be a good place for Barlow and me.

AT THE END OF THE WEEK, BARLOW SAID, "WHAT SHALL IT BE?" He was dressing for work. This was the day they'd promised to decide about selling the mine.

"I know this much; I want a different life for you. No more wrangling with the association, worrying about shipping and how you'll pay the company's bills."

"And I want an easier life for you."

"I'm not sure I need an easier life." If we left, I might stop worrying about the dangers of mining and the hardships of miners' families. Barlow held out his wrists and I buttoned his cuffs. "We need to move forward in faith," I said.

He held me close. "But in what direction?"

"We shouldn't go somewhere just to get away. I mean, the place we decide to go should offer something more, shouldn't it?"

"That sounds wise."

"And how do we know before we experience it?"

"May Rose, I think you don't want to leave Winkler."

I did not want to make him stay. "We've both moved more than once, and I think uprooting must always be difficult. But I don't know if either of us could tolerate living here if the mine is run by a bad operator. On the other hand, I'd like you to work less. We don't need a big house; we could live simply."

He kissed my forehead. "There might be a way."

CHAPTER 24

Marriage eases a person's troubles in one sense and doubles them in another. I'd had my ups and downs, but now I experienced Barlow's as well, much as he tried to hide them.

The day he and his partners were to meet with Hollis Stone, I was useless for work. I felt like I might be doing everything for the last time, soaking in my view of the mountains, passing the time of day with my neighbors. In the house, I hovered close to Freddy as he tried to climb on the furniture, and I ran to the front window at the approach of every passing vehicle to see if it contained the man who wanted to buy our mine.

Luzanna was full of her own apprehensions. We'd moved the washing machine to the back porch for the summer, and I took Freddy outside while she pinned the bachelors' laundry to my clotheslines.

"I know I have to let Alma go. It's right, ain't it? There's no future for her here. But she could take an examination and teach in our school. I think she would do that, if the Walker boy hadn't gone away. Or if she'd had a chance with Jonah Watson or that poor soldier boy. Sometimes I think she wants to get away so she don't end up like me."

"Luzanna, you've said yourself that our children have to prove they don't need us. They don't hold on to that notion forever— just until they get older and have responsibilities. Then they're glad to lean on us."

"Like Wanda," she said.

"Like Wanda. As for Alma, I think she knows some boy could come along and change her life in a minute. But for now, we need to be proud, because she wants to change it herself."

I sat on the back step, brushing away flies and watching Freddy toddle precariously on the uneven ground. His head was no longer bald, but covered with light-colored curls. When he fell on his rear, I stood to help him up, but he swatted his hand to warn me away.

"Look at him," Luzanna said. "Already he wants to be on his own."

"Oh, no." I sat down again, suddenly weak.

"Why, May Rose." Luzanna leaned back with a wide-eyed look. "You're expecting again!"

I placed my hand on my flat belly. "Does it show?"

"Up here's where I see it," Luzanna said, waving a hand across her own chest. "Does Barlow know?"

I started to cry.

"Oh, dear, he'll be glad of it, and the second's always easier... it's all right, honey, everything will be all right. I'll be with you."

I cried harder.

⚙️

I FELT BETTER AS SOON AS I SAW BARLOW'S FACE. FREDDY latched onto his leg, and he swept him up and pulled me into their hug. "We said no to Stone, and I've agreed to sell to Will and Randolph. We can stay or go wherever you'd like. But not until fall—I can't leave until I establish a business manager in my place."

"So come fall, you'll work no more?"

"I'll need to occupy myself with something. We'll figure it out."

Freddy wiggled to be set down. "This boy has his own ideas," Barlow said.

"I wish Hester could see him. But maybe she can. Living here, I often feel her with us, even though everything is so changed from what it was. Even the river has found a different course."

"You don't want to leave."

"It's true. And it's my turn to have an idea. Is it too late to take a walk?"

In the last hour of daylight we explored the place where we'd met, the site of Hester's boardinghouse.

"This feels like home," I said. The site was now a field of winter-brown weeds, but sprouts of green were shooting up between them. Only a few stones of the foundation peeked from the ground.

I took a step from the street into the weeds. "The ground is wet," Barlow said. "You'll muddy your shoes and soil your dress."

"Come on."

Barlow lifted Freddy from his stroller and we stepped carefully, reminding each other of the location of the apple tree and the iron fence, and how the boardinghouse had sat relative to everything else.

Barlow looked back at the hillside of company houses. "Hester and I saw newspaper photos after the fires. I'm still amazed when I think how Will cleaned all that up."

From this spot I had a view of the river that was not blocked by the railyard. "If a house were set farther back from the road with a long lawn and a few trees in front, it would not catch so much dust and smoke," I said.

"Is that what you're thinking? This is where you want to build our house?"

"Not just a house. Why not a boardinghouse?"

His glance was like a test to see if I was serious. "Not for the bachelors," he said.

"No, for visitors, and maybe a teacher or two. I believe there's no such establishment in any of the mining towns nearby. Do you think Will would sell this land to us?"

"For you, he might make it a gift." Barlow let his eyes roam over the landscape. I saw his interest struggle with his natural reluctance to hope too much.

"This is what I want," I said.

He put his free arm around my shoulders. "In that case..."

With every step toward home, I went over in my mind the features of the boardinghouse as it had been and as I wanted to see it again. Exactly the same.

THE BOARDINGHOUSE

BOOK 5 IN THE MOUNTAIN WOMEN SERIES

Stronger together.

May Rose has the husband, family, and boardinghouse she wanted, but managing business and doing her best for loved ones make challenging days and anxious nights. Now her husband is ailing, someone from the past is trying to find her, and malicious guests are poised to ruin her reputation.

But she's not alone.

As she does her duty and stands up for herself, she's strengthened by the love and support of family and friends.

The Boardinghouse is the fifth novel in the Mountain Women Series, presenting the struggles, triumphs, friendships and loves of women in a small West Virginia town in the early 1900s.

Look for *The Boardinghouse* on Amazon.

ABOUT THE AUTHOR

I've been lucky. Years ago, I wanted to live on a farm, and my husband said "Let's do it." When personal computers were introduced, I wanted to know about them and own one, and lucky me, the school where I taught offered a course in Basic. When we bought our first computer, I discovered the writer's best friend--word processing. Before that, I could not write without crossing out most of a typewritten or handwritten page, and progress seemed impossible. When I wanted to shift from teaching to writing, the first Macintosh computers came out, and I was lucky enough to have, along with technical and business writing, the first "desktop publishing" service in my area. And when finally I had the leisure to give a lot of time to a novel, my husband didn't merely tolerate my commitment, he encouraged it.

Inspiration for the Mountain Women series came first from the mountain wilderness, both beautiful and challenging for those who live there. I appreciated accounts of early 20th century life and industry, the forerunners of today's technology and culture. When I read Roy B. Clarkson's non-fiction account of lumbering in West Virginia, (Tumult on the Mountain, 1964, McClain Printing Co., Parsons, WV), with more than 250 photos of giant trees, loggers, sawmills, trains, and towns, I found the setting for the first book in the series. Finally, I was inspired by men and women of previous generations who faced difficulties unknown today. Researching and writing these novels, I have felt closer to the lives of grandparents I never knew.

Learn more about author Carol Ervin at http://www.carolervin.com

facebook.com/carolervin.author

amazon.com/stores/Carol-Ervin/author/B0094IOERY

bookbub.com/authors/carol-ervin

ALSO BY CAROL ERVIN

The Mountain Women Series

The Girl on the Mountain

Cold Comfort

Midwinter Sun

The Women's War

The Boardinghouse

Kith and Kin

Fools for Love

The Meaning of Us

Hearts and Souls

The Promise of Mondays

Pressing On

Down in the Valley

Rona's House

A Novella, Prequel to the Mountain Women Series

For the Love of Jamie Long

A Christmas Novella

Christmas with Charlie

Other Novels

Ridgetop

Dell Zero

ACKNOWLEDGMENTS

Thanks to author friend Bob Summer and to Diane Plotts, Michele Moore and Carol A. Martin for your careful reading and excellent suggestions.